No... ...g...tt
and the
Dog-People

BY THE SAME AUTHOR

For readers aged 15+

Desiccation

Noah Padgett
and the
Dog-People

Sarah Potter

ISBN: 978-1536973488
ISBN: 1536973483

Acknowledgements

Thank you to beta reader Leigh Ward-Smith for casting her eagle eye over the penultimate draft of *Noah Padgett and the Dog-People.* Thank you to Zachary Ashford and Joshua Munns for their enthusiastic and encouraging feedback on the first draft. Thank you to my husband, Victor, for designing the book cover and surviving the experience. Thank you to a certain chocolate Labrador puppy for inspiring me to write the novel and for supervising me throughout the creative process.

Contents

— CHAPTER ONE —

Trash and Click

Noah flies along the pavement, weaving and dodging shoppers, pushchairs, and old women with walking frames. He's already nearly two hours late home, so he doesn't need the entire population of Brighton and every tourist in the universe getting in his way.

Trust his stepmother, Kate, to have gone off the grid all afternoon and not picked up the house phone or her mobile, either to him or to the school office.

'Snarky' Bannister, the sports teacher, who demands all the boys call him 'Sir', kept him back from school, yet again. Some kids are born athletic and some are not, and Noah with his lack of co-ordination is definitely a *not*. To make matters worse, he's scared of heights and his refusal to climb the ropes in the gym has become an issue between him and Snarky.

Today, he braved the climb halfway, panicked, and gave himself rope-burn of the inner thighs during his uncontrolled descent. As Noah sat there nursing his injuries and daring to shed a tear or two, Snarky said,

'It's time you manned yourself up, Padgett,' and rewarded him with an after-school detention for cowardice.

Still, Snarky seems a kitten compared to Kate, the sabre-toothed tigress who's sure to tear him to shreds when he gets home.

He takes a short cut across the rec. A couple of boys from his school are half-heartedly kicking a football about. Others are lounging on the ground, littering the grass with bottles, tins, chocolate bar wrappers, and crisp packets. They ignore Noah and he ignores them.

Boiled and near to throwing up, he rounds the corner to his house, hits the front drive at full-tilt, and skids to a halt on the gravel. No car. He punches the air and shouts, "Yes!" Kate is out. For a moment he's jubilant, until it strikes him that she's always threatening to get rid of his puppy. What if she has gone and done it, because he wasn't back in time to walk Bluebell?

His hand is shaking so much it takes several tries before he gets his key into the lock and opens the front door. Once inside, he slams the door shut behind him and slings his backpack on the hall floor. The grandfather clock strikes five o'clock. A long silence follows. The house stinks of puppy, but there's not a squeak out of her.

He legs it through to the utility room, hoping he'll find an angelic chocolate Labrador curled up snoozing in her pen, which is where Kate shuts her when no-one is at home, except this isn't where she is now.

Bluebell has chewed through the wooden bars and gone mountaineering over the kitchen table and trashed the kitchen. Noah clutches at his head and lets out a long groan. Helpless, he gawps at the smashed cereal bowls, a licked-clean butter dish, tipped over chairs, and the shredded remains of a cornflake packet. Kate must have been out on one of her all-day shopping trips, leaving Bluebell on her own all day.

From upstairs, come crashes and thumps similar to the ones Dad makes when he kicks off his work shoes in the evenings and hurls them at the wardrobe. Bluebell starts to bark and clatter against a distant door.

Noah scrambles up the stairs, his arms tangling with his legs and his head exploding with fear. He can see it already, his stepmother's dressing room: that shrine to shopping with its wall-to-wall wardrobes and a floor-to-ceiling shoe rack threatening to overbalance and crush Bluebell to death.

The door at the end of the landing has a ceramic nameplate on it. He often dreams of vandalising this nameplate. Today, when he arrives at it, he averts his eyes from the words 'Kate's Room' painted in fancy black letters surrounded by pink roses. Anybody would think the dressing room belonged to a six-year-old girl, rather than a regular Cruella de Ville.

He sweeps his sweat-soaked fringe back off his forehead, wipes his clammy hands on his school trousers, and takes a few deep breaths. Bluebell has stopped barking and other noises jump to the fore. The downstairs clock ticks. A tap drips. A twig scratches against the outside of a window. A buzzing insect collides with glass. Someone has a mower going. The girls next door are having a squawk, and for once he'd rather be out there with them.

He counts down from ten to one and barges into the room before he loses his nerve. Bluebell greets him with multiple lickings and vertical take-offs. He stands there horror-struck, with his heart taking such a dive it almost drops out of him and lands at his feet with a splat.

3

The once brilliant-white carpet has had an argument with the colour yellow. The lemony patches are part of an alien landscape strewn with mangled strips of leather, rubber, plastic, velvet, tapestry fabric, pink fluff, buckles, buttons, and sequins. The lowest twenty slots of the shoe rack are accusing black voids. Noah visualises himself in disgrace and penniless misery for the rest of his childhood as he fights to pay Kate back with money from a paper round. 'Oh, Bluebell, what have you done?' He wrestles her into his arms, frantic to escape the nightmare.

But after he has turned to leave, he suffers an overpowering urge to look behind him. It feels as though some crazed scientist has messed with reality and stuffed sixty seconds into two, so a couple of time-strands become one.

A Saluki dog dressed in hot pants, sequin top, and stiletto heels is standing upright on her long back legs in the middle of the dressing room. The flaxen-haired, black-snouted beauty waves at Noah with a paw-hand, her claws painted with pink-glitter nail polish. 'Hi there,' she says, before vanishing into the full-length wardrobe mirror.

When time returns to normal, Bluebell wriggles free and rushes to the mirror, pressing her nose to it and steaming up the glass. She wags her tail and woofs at her own reflection, as if she's inviting the dog-girl to return for a further game of 'let's trash Kate's shrine'.

After an agonised wait, Noah hears the slow crunch of the Range Rover's tyres on the driveway. Hiding in his bedroom with Bluebell, he does not realise Kate has let herself in the house until she passes his door with a rustle of shopping bags.

The familiar routine, he thinks, but today it has a scarier scenario. If this was a computer game, he would choose this moment to beam up to another planet in another solar system on the other side of the galaxy, taking Bluebell with him.

Kate's dressing room door creaks open. Stunned silence. The thud-thud-thud-thud of shopping bags slipping from her hands on to the carpet. A scream, shrill enough to break every window in the road. A wailing. 'No, my shoes—my beautiful shoes.' And the chilling words. 'I'm going to kill that puppy. Throttle her with my bare hands. Feed her to the crows.'

Noah seeks refuge with Bluebell under his duvet, fighting the desire to throw up. He can taste sour chocolate from the snack he ate while rushing home from school in a stress. Kate hurtles back along the landing, letting out dramatic sobs, and crashes through his bedroom door, nearly knocking it off its hinges. She stands there, white-faced, and rakes her fingernails through her short dark hair, her red lipsticky mouth drawn tight across her teeth. She reminds Noah of a wild animal grooming itself before battle. There is not a genuine tear in sight to soften her hard, black eyes. Just dry rage.

Hugging Bluebell close to him, Noah snatches up his water pistol from his bedside table and squirts it at Kate's face, straight into her eyes. She rubs furiously at her eyelids, smudging her mascara and streaking her face with green slime. Only then does he remember the pistol contains stagnant water taken from a vase of dead flowers. He had put it there a couple of weeks ago, when he and his friend George were fooling about with some old kiddie toys. Even though he hates his stepmother, Noah wouldn't want to blind her. He's in a real panic now, but there's no way he will say sorry to her, ever.

Kate glares at him out of streaming red eyes, with her arms drawn down to her sides. She clenches, unclenches, and re-clenches her hands. They are tense and bony—almost bird claws. 'The puppy goes tomorrow—first thing, no argument.'

'Goes where?'

'I don't care. The vets, the breeder, the Battersea Dog's Home, wherever, as long as it's a million miles from me.'

'B-b-but you can't just get rid of her. She has feelings.'

Kate curls her lips in a sneer. 'I have feelings too, which your father's chosen to ignore. He knows I can't stand dogs, yet he gives you a nasty, messy, puppy for your birthday. This is as much his fault as yours.'

At ten minutes to nine, Dad returns from London. 'I'm starving,' he tells an empty hall.

No reply.

He tries again. 'Is anyone at home?'

Noah hears him walking around, talking to himself, trying doors to various rooms until finally he finds Kate. She's in the telly room directly beneath Noah's bedroom, doubtless stationed there so he won't miss any of what she has to say to Dad. Her slights such as 'your son this', 'evil puppy that', and 'useless husband other' sound set to go on into infinity.

Normally, Noah would drown out one of his stepmother's rants by playing some heavy metal on his iPod, but he needs to listen out for Bluebell, whom Kate has banished to the conservatory.

At five minutes past ten, Dad manages to escape to Noah's room. He dumps a bottle of cola on the bedside

6

table, along with a large bag of crisps and a couple of doughnuts 'Wouldn't want you starving to death, mate.'

Dad helps himself to a doughnut and collapses down onto the end of Noah's bed. He looks shattered after a day of trading on the stock market. His hair is all dishevelled, his face pinched and pale, and he seems thinner than usual. He's still wearing his tie, although it's loosened and crooked, and his shirt has a couple of missing buttons. There are also some fresh scratch marks just beneath his neck, which Noah guesses are Kate's doing.

She shrieks up the stairs. 'Get down here this minute, Craig, or you can sleep in the garden shed tonight. Your son's a disgrace.'

Dad drags himself up off the bed. He has white sugar on his cheek and a bit of jam on his upper lip like a toddler. 'Don't worry,' he says, with a sad but guilty look to his face. 'I'll keep an eye out for Bluebell and do my best to sweeten up your mother.'

'She isn't my mother, so don't call her that.' He really wishes Dad would get the message and stop trying to play happy families.

As World War Three breaks out downstairs, all Noah can think of is poor Bluebell stuck there in the conservatory on her own, quivering and whimpering in a corner, not understanding what's going on.

At a quarter-to-eleven, after Kate has finished breaking every piece of china downstairs, she stomps upstairs. Noah flicks off his light, tosses a sweatshirt over his computer monitor, and holds his breath. Kate marches past his room, rattling the door in its frame, tutting and huffing to herself. Dad trudges along the landing after her, muttering swear words.

Kate shouts at him from the en-suite bathroom: all

7

her usual stuff about his not bothering hanging up his clothes and leaving shaving bristles in the hand basin, as well as her making vicious digs about his rough upbringing on a London council estate. Never mind that he's smart and has done well for himself.

Noah knows he has taken after Dad and is smart too, although he can't find the motivation to work hard these days. However well he does, his stepmother will find nothing good to say about him. His sole crime is his close resemblance to his real mum, and the only way he could change this would be to dye his blond hair purple, grows his fringe down to his chin to cover up his hazel eyes, and eat mountains of junk food to turn him from skinny to fat. Not one week passes without Kate accusing Dad of loving 'that rough Peckham girl' more than her. How stupid being jealous of a dead person.

Her words now reach Noah's ears in fits and starts. It sounds as if she's brushing her teeth and shouting through thick foam. Perhaps she will swallow too much fluoride and poison herself.

At last she runs out of steam and silence reigns over the house.

<><><>

It is twenty minutes to midnight. Noah peers out from behind the kitchen door into the empty hall. The white-light of a full moon shines through the frosted glass of the stair-window and the house vibrates from Dad's monstrous snores. Noah bets Kate is lying there next to Dad wide-awake, fuming.

He carries Bluebell upstairs, doing his best to walk on tiptoe at the same time. He's determined she'll spend her last night in his company. On the landing, she starts wriggling and squeaking. He makes a dash for it, with one hand clamping her jaw shut. Once inside his room,

8

he sits on the bed stroking her, hoping to calm them both. Random thoughts tumble about in his mind—all of them bad—but at least Bluebell can enjoy her remaining time with him, in happy ignorance of her future. She crashes out on her back, fast asleep with her two front paws around her nose.

Seeking a diversion from misery, Noah creeps across the room to his computer, only to find it has gone into hibernation. He attempts to reboot the stupid machine but the following error message comes up on the screen:

     ◦*System restart has been paused:*

     ◦*Continue with system restart.*

     ◦*Delete restoration data and proceed to system boot menu.*

He bangs his fist down on the desk in frustration, waking Bluebell, who rushes across the room, keen for a bit of excitement. Scooping her off the floor onto his lap without paying her proper attention, he tries to decide what to do next. As his finger hovers over the mouse-button, Bluebell wags her tail and nibbles at the sleeve of his T-shirt.

'Naughty puppy, let me concentrate.' He keeps his eyes fixed on the monitor. But Bluebell seems determined to have a game with him, and nips him on the thigh just below the hem of his boxer shorts. This distracts him for a few seconds as he checks for broken skin. During this time, Bluebell strikes the keyboard with her paw.

The error message disappears and the screen starts to fill with angry black clouds. These clouds have a ravenous appearance to them and look ready to devour every file and programme on the computer, including schoolwork and saved games.

Noah's pulse runs out of control and his armpits draw instant sweat. Even Bluebell raises her hackles in alarm. The clouds pile on top of each other in a relentless forward march, but instead of Noah's computer crashing as he expects, the clouds suddenly go into mind-blowing reversal on the screen, drawing him with them.

His brain feels as though it's disappearing down a plughole, with reality fighting to retrieve him before he disappears out of reach around the bend in the pipe.

Bluebell cranes her neck forward and her brown nose touches the screen.

The clouds part to reveal the words…

www.zyx-dimension.com
(Double click on the above link for further information)

— CHAPTER TWO —

Labrador in a Red-checked Shirt

The hall clock strikes midnight. Noah counts its chimes from one to twelve. He tells himself the ravenous clouds are just a preview to a fantasy game: that there's no harm in checking things out.

He clicks on the link.

The screen shimmers, liquefies, and starts to drag Bluebell through into a chemical soup spiced with lead and mercury. Noah grabs hold of her shoulders to haul her back, his whole body torn by panic. But the liquid tide snatches him, too, and spits him out into a vast wind tunnel, which sucks him and Bluebell up with the force of a tornado. Stretched out thin, his ears popping, Noah gasps for breath and squeezes his eyes shut against the stinging air.

He lands with a splash in cold water, loses his hold on Bluebell, and sinks. Pondweed wraps around his neck. He thrashes his arms around, convinced he's drowning. Forcing his eyes open to get his bearings, he discovers he's sitting on the bottom of what looks like a pond.

As Bluebell doggy-paddles away from him at speed, caught up with the joy of finding her swimming legs, Noah wills her to pick up his distress signals. He knows she's strong enough to rescue him, despite her small size; only a few days ago, she dragged a heavy hose-reel by her teeth all the way up the garden path at the side of the house, plus, she's impossible to beat at tug-of-war.

His lungs burn as he draws the last drop of air from them. Fireworks explode in his head. He needs to breathe … needs, needs, needs to breathe.

Water tumbles into his lungs. It is a billion times worse than choking on cola. He's drowning in his computer while his puppy swims in the opposite direction. His chest is on the point of exploding and his spine snapping. Then an odd tranquillity comes over him. He sees the smiling face of his real mum, Shelley, floating before him. She's a beacon lighting his way to the afterlife.

'Thing, wake up,' says a deep, barking voice. Noah wonders if it's the voice of God calling to him down a tunnel.

Next, he feels a mouth with loads of teeth over his mouth. It blows air into him, with a breath smelling so gross, even the water in his lungs wants to escape from it. He changes his mind about it being God.

Someone hauls him up from behind into a sitting position. He coughs, splutters, and pukes in the long grass. When he has finished puking, he says, 'Ouch, your nails are digging into me.'

His rescuer lets out a chuckle of sorts. 'How about a little bit of gratitude?'

'Yeah, th…' Noah's voice trails off. His brain feels disconnected from his body, as if he has left his head floating behind him in the water.

He squints across the huge lake into a low, deep-orange sun. There's nothing to measure his direction by, so it's impossible to know if he has arrived in early morning or early evening. The ducks are going a dabbling, tails up in the weeds; a gentle breeze ripples the lake.

Noah turns to face his rescuer for the first time, intending to ask after Bluebell but instead finding himself gaping in astonishment. A dog-man sits there, upright as a human. He has the butch face of an elderly black Labrador—grey muzzle, yellow teeth, kind brown eyes, ears alert, expression questioning—but he wears a red-checked shirt, old corduroy tan trousers, and thigh-high green wading wellies.

The Labrador-man takes a packet of tobacco out of his shirt pocket and packs some of it into a briar pipe, using his super-elongated pads, opposable thumbs, and flattened claws. He delves into his left trouser pocket and extracts one item after another, chucking each of them on the ground. These include a couple of brightly coloured fishing floats, a dirty old handkerchief, a bunch of keys, and some boiled sweets in wrappers. At last, he finds what he is looking for. 'Got you—dry as a bone. What a mercy and oh so sweet. A dog without a light for his pipe is a very sore dog indeed.'

Now I know I'm dead, thinks Noah. He wonders if Mum had the same experience after her car flew off a bridge and she drowned.

<><><>

It is night. Noah awakens to find himself lying on a makeshift bed, although he has no memory of having fallen asleep. Propping himself up on one elbow, he sees a moon has risen over the lake and thrown a

13

shimmering cloak over its surface. The reflection of its face shifts about, reminding Noah of a huge version of the white opal pendant his mum used to wear and the way it swayed when she leant forward to tie his shoelaces before he could tie them himself. Night crickets chirrup. An owl shrieks nearby. Another owl answers with a gentle woo-woo from further off. The water of the lake laps against the low bank of its shoreline.

A smell of cooking fish reaches him. He drags himself up off his bed and stumbles over to join Labrador-man by a campfire. They are in the middle of a glade, well away from the water's edge. Labrador-man has skewered three whole fish on a long spike and is cooking them over the fire. Beyond him, lies a log cabin. Beyond this, the trees of a forest stand straight as guards, their uppermost branches silvered by the moonlight into polished spiked helmets.

Noah's mind is still in shock, much of it a blank.

'Is people-person feeling better for his sleep?' asks Labrador-man.

'I'm called Noah Padgett,' he says, relieved to remember his own name.

'I'm Graham Labrador.'

'That's cool.'

'What do you call your little four-paw walker friend?' asks Graham. 'Every time I speak to her, she woofs at me.'

Jolted out of his partial amnesia, Noah leaps to his feet. 'She's alive? You've spoken to her?'

'Sure, although such an awkward way of walking about, I never did see.'

Noah lurches about the glade, shouting in every direction. 'Bluebell … Bluebell … Bluebell.' His puppy zooms out through the open door of the cabin to him. She leaps about, squeaking, licking, chewing, rolling on her back and wetting herself. Noah has never felt so overjoyed to see anyone in his life.

Graham finishes cooking the fish, pulls them off the skewers one at a time, and puts them on three tin plates with a serving each of chopped vegetables and herbs dressed in oil. When the Labrador-man passes one of the plates to Bluebell, Noah snatches it away and does his best to fillet the fish. Once he has removed the majority of bones, Bluebell launches herself at her food and polishes it off in a blink.

With his head on one side and ears raised, Graham appears unimpressed.

'What's bugging you?' Noah asks.

'Well, I'm all for allowing pups a certain amount of self-expression, but they do need a bit of discipline, too.'

Noah hugs Bluebell close and scowls at Graham.

The dog-man shrugs his shoulders. 'Never mind. Eat up your food before it gets cold.'

Noah decides fish and vegetables taste far more delicious eaten out in the fresh air than at the kitchen table or in the dining room back home. No indigestion either, from having to suffer Dad and Kate having one of their arguments while he tries to enjoy his meal.

Graham hums to himself as he discards the fish bones from their meal into the fire. He takes the dirty dishes and cutlery down to the lakeside to wash them. Bluebell wriggles out of Noah's arms to follow him. She wades about in the shallows, lapping at the water.

The moon is high above the lake and white as Wensleydale cheese. It has no darkened areas to its surface to show meteorite damage, as on the Earth's moon, nor cloud formations to suggest a protective atmosphere. Whichever way he looks at it, Noah reckons it a scientific puzzle.

<><><>

Bluebell sits on her haunches, howling up at the sky. The orange sun of yesterday seems to have turned into a candy-pink one: either this, or there are twin suns with slightly different rising and setting times. Noah rubs at his eyes, to make sure he isn't imagining things, but the pink sun stays put.

He lets out a loud yawn and Bluebell comes bounding over. They go to the lakeside to see Graham, who's wading in its shallows with a fishing rod in his hands.

'Good afternoon, young people-person,' says Labrador-man.

Noah wonders if, other than Graham, there are other strangely evolved creatures in this twin-sun world. The birds, squirrels, and fish seem normal enough. Noah wants to ask Graham outright if he's a freak of nature, but manages to come up with a more tactful question. 'Are there any others people-persons like me round here?'

'Nope.'

'Not in towns?'

'Nope.'

'How about zoos?'

'Nope.'

<><><>

Bluebell wanders off a short distance, on the trail of a scent. When she reaches the edge of the glade, she sniffs about in some rough grass. Beyond her, sunlight dances amongst the forest's trees. It's a peaceful and idyllic scene, thinks Noah, suspecting it won't last. And his pessimism is well founded.

16

From close by, a shrill whistle sounds, followed by the clop-crunch of heavy boots running along, crushing twigs underfoot. Noah leaps to attention a second before a grey wolf-man—wearing an old-fashioned military red coat—dashes between the trees.

A blackbird lets out a sharp warning call. A squirrel darts up an oak tree and stays there, tucked into a high up crook with its nose poking out. Bluebell rolls on her back to chew a stick.

Noah walks towards her, trying to look relaxed, but his legs are shaking. She stays on her back, watching him out of one eye. When he's within two arms' lengths of her, she jumps up onto all fours and invites him to play tug-of-war. As he reaches out his hand, intending to grab the stick and pull Bluebell away to safety, a butterfly flutters in front of her eyes. It darts off deep amongst the trees, with Bluebell in speedy pursuit, heading straight towards where Noah saw the wolf-man. There are other dog-soldiers running between the trees now, but dressed in dull greens and browns. The sunlight glints upon their weapons.

Terror binds Noah to the spot. The glade is too big, and he a powerless dot in its centre. The trees seem to have grown faces. He snatches a desperate look back at Graham, who appears to be fast asleep in his tree-hammock, with a battered old felt hat covering his eyes and snout.

Noah calls quietly, fighting to keep fear from his voice. 'Bluebell, Bluebell.'

She stops and stares at him, and wags her tail.

Noah pats the ground with his hand. 'Come on, girl. Come Bluebell, come.'

She sits down on her haunches and shuffles backwards, flicking the tip of her tail and letting out small barks. As a last resort, Noah flops over on his back and plays dead, which does the trick. She runs straight to him and starts licking his face.

Grasping her, before she can escape again, he clambers to his feet and bombs over to Graham. With a squirming Bluebell tucked under one arm, he shakes the dog-man, pinches him, knocks his hat off, lifts his earflap, and yells in his lughole to wake up, but Graham just lets out an extra loud snore and carries on sleeping.

Noah hates leaving him, but protecting Bluebell is more important. He locks her in his arms and runs for the nearest shelter: an outdoor loo built of concrete with a solid wooden door and a five-lever lock. Some very large spiders live inside the loo, their larder well stocked with fly carcasses. Noah sees them as the least of his worries.

He shuts the door behind him and engages the lock, throwing himself into a false twilight. Clambering up onto the loo seat, he fights the spiders' dust-filled webs to look out of the small, high up window. Bluebell stands with her front paws on the seat, whining, and wagging her tail. When he ignores her, she takes advantage of his shoeless state by chewing at what is left of his socks.

The window is filthy. He spits at the glass and rubs off some dirt to make a spy hole, but still cannot see much. There isn't a lot to hear either, with the window jammed shut and its latch rusted solid.

If this was a fantasy scenario, thinks Noah, he would have a selection of magical weapons to use. Or perhaps it really is a fantasy scenario but in a nightmare caused by an overdose of computer games. He mutters under his breath. 'Please don't let this be real. Please let me wake up in my bed at home.'

But no awakening comes. Just fear prickling his whole body.

A creature scrabbles and claws against the outside of the loo door. The knob rattles. Someone whispers; another replies.

Noah clenches his jaw and his breath comes out in shallow pants. Bluebell starts to whine again, louder than before, her tail thumping. She looks up at him out of questioning eyes.

More whispering … short silence … then an almighty thudding from some sort of battering ram. The door shakes in its frame and releases a few tiny splinters. Noah takes a sharp intake of breath at the sound of each blow. Further splinters: the air smells of stale pee; his eyes sting and his head swims.

He finds it hard to believe the door can hold firm under such an assault. Surely, any minute it will cave in, or split in two? He counts the blows. One, two, three, four, five, six, seven, eight, nine, ten, eleven—still it stands. Twelve, thirteen, fourteen—despite a cracking, rending noise, it refuses to fall apart.

A heated swearing match starts up outside. One of the voices is harsh as a machine gun and the other sounds as if the owner's throat is full of gravel. They are arguing about whose fault it is the chosen log was not strong enough. In the end, they agree neither of them is to blame; the log is rotten inside, but not so rotten they can't use the broken pieces to beat up their subordinates and show them who's still in charge.

Tortured howls and yelps fill the air. When the assault comes to an abrupt halt, Noah tightens in dread and forgets to breathe, convinced it will be his and Bluebell's turn next.

After a few seconds of nothing happening, Gravel-voice lets out a gritty laugh. His companions join in, their laughter sounding forced and most likely a case of them having to see the joke or risk further beatings.

After their laughter has dried up, the deranged troop marches away, singing a rude song in two-time.

Noah slumps down on the loo seat and lifts Bluebell onto his lap. He trembles from head to foot. A deep silence descends upon the forest, almost quiet enough to hear the spiders weave their webs. No bird-song. No wind in the trees. No buzz of insects. Bluebell quivers beneath his hands, her little heart pitter-pattering against her ribcage as fast as summer rain on an iron roof. He strokes her, while listening out for the enemy's return.

Nothing happens for such an age, Noah wonders if it's safe to go outside. In answer to his thought, a rock smashes through the window and lands on his head. Stars explode behind his eyes. Thick, pungent smoke starts to fill the confined space. Bluebell leaps off his lap and jumps about, barking at the smoke.

Noah's head seems to disconnect from his neck and his brain suffers a violent shaking. Overwhelmed with giddiness, he tips off the loo seat and smashes the side of his forehead into the concrete wall.

— CHAPTER THREE —

Sergeant Salt and His Lurcher Infantry Band

Noah has never experienced such pain. Someone might as well be thwacking the crown of his head with a timpani mallet, mistaking it for a kettledrum. He lies flat on his back, imprisoned on a pallet constructed of woven sticks. Ropes tie his ankles together and criss-cross the upper half of his body, pinning his arms to his sides. A metal bracket secures each of his wrists.

He can see the lake out of the corner of one eye; out of the other, he can see Graham's empty hammock. Above him, angry rain clouds pile into a blue patch of sky, threatening to turn on their taps and drench him.

Straining at the ropes without effect, he suddenly remembers something Kate did when she was stuck in a too-tight dress. She shrank down her hands, by tucking her thumbs and three shortest fingers under her middle fingers, and then slithered out of the dress, making each hand snake its way out of the sleeves. He had always thought it stupid of her to buy dresses a couple of sizes too small when she owned so many that fitted her okay. For once, he's thankful for his stepmother's stupidity.

He tests one metal bracket with a bit of shrinking and wriggling of his right hand, stopping abruptly when Gravel-voice lets out a sudden shout from nearby. Terrified he is about to be beaten for trying to escape, Noah bites his own tongue and draws blood. But it is just some joke about how many poodles it takes to change a light bulb that has started Gravel-voice off, although Noah misses the punch line, what with all the coarse laughter.

A rich aroma of cooking starts to fill the air. Smoke from a fire spirals upwards to blend with the dark sky. To Noah's relief, Bluebell lets out a few barks. She sounds hungry and frustrated, rather than in pain. Gravel-voice swears at her and calls her 'four-legged mutant'. This makes her bark even louder. He roars at her. 'Shut it or I'll roast you and eat you.'

'You'd get gut ache, scoffing the likes of her,' suggests someone.

'Percival won't pay us, either,' says another, of more refined tone.

'Shut it, clot-brained cretins, you,' says Gravel-voice. 'You ain't to say nuffink, you hear me? Just shut your stinking traps.'

Mr Refined speaks again. 'You ever heard of dog eats dog? Percival's one brand of scumbag, and we're another. At this point in time he's the highest bidder, but our loyalty costs triple.'

'How much did this Percival fellow pay you?' This last question belongs to Graham Labrador.

Inspired at hearing him so close by, Noah manages to free his right-hand from its metal restraint without further effort.

'Old fellow, I don't recall anyone giving you permission to speak,' says Mr Refined.

'Yeah, button it,' says another.

'I've got three grand to spare in my bank account,' says Graham.

This comment promotes a total breakdown of order.

'Three grand!'

'Three grand? Who's he think we is?'

'Lucky if we got a month's worth of beer out of that.'

'Bleeding insult.'

Whilst they are busy sneering at Graham, Noah frees his left-hand. Now he must apply Kate's too-tight dress-removal principles yet again, this time by *thinking* his body smaller so he can complete his escape.

To thin himself, Noah tries to imagine he is a cartoon character flattened by a steamroller. He twists and turns his cartoon-self from side to side, working hard to ignore the scratch and burn of the rope-fibres through his semi-shredded T-shirt. When the ropes have loosened up a little, he pulls his arms and shoulders in, prays nobody is looking his way, and squirms downwards, out from under the rope.

It takes him a couple of minutes to stir up the courage to lift his head and check out what is going on. It is not a happy sight, with Bluebell shut in a cage and Graham sitting on a kitchen-style chair, his wrists bound to the chair's back and his ankles tied to its legs.

Their captors are a motley crew of a dozen or so mangy, coarse-coated mongrel-types, dressed in mix-and-match, dull muddy green, brown, or grey ragged military uniforms. Only one of them stands out as different, with his tight-fitting scarlet coat, black three-cornered hat, and grubby white breeches. The outfit reminds Noah of a picture in one of his school history books of an early nineteenth-century British infantryman.

Scarlet-coat, as if sensing Noah is watching him, sharply rotates his head in his direction. Noah lies down, closes his eyes, and holds his breath.

Noah sits thinking, while tied back-to-back with Graham. He bets scarlet-coated Sergeant Salt doesn't miss a trick—in particular, tricks performed by boys copying Houdini—which was why he kept him apart from Graham earlier, to stop them plotting.

One of the greens has a single eye trained upon Noah. A grubby patch covers the other eye. If Noah dares to fidget, or glance too far to the left or right, One-eye clears his throat and lifts up his patch to reveal a still grubbier empty eye socket.

A short distance away, within his direct line of vision, Noah can now see three other dog-men dressed in bright coloured military-style coats: a yellow, a sky-blue, and a bright pink.

'The LIMS rank system, from major down to private, is one big joke at the expense of the Zyx Dimension Imperial Army,' says Salt. 'And the ZDIA takes itself very seriously indeed.'

Noah guesses this is Salt's idea of starting a conversation with him. Rather than risk the wrong words, Noah grunts in reply while attempting to hold his breath against the stink arising from the sergeant's rough, terrier-like, dark-grey hair.

Some soldiers prepare a meal over the fire by barbecuing a variety of wildlife on the blades of their bayonets without any care for the basic rules of hygiene.

Food leftovers and general grime encrust their paw-hands and their weapons. Bluebell wags her tail and barks louder. Hint. Hint.

'Shut it, you fickle puppy,' Noah tells her.

'You talking to me, mutant?' asks one of the cooks.

'Why? Are *you* a puppy?' Noah replies, before he can stop himself.

'A puppy? Baldy squirt, there ain't puppies in the LIMs. I ain't in need of bitch's milk and I ain't putting up with your mouth. Shut it, or I'll cut your tongue out and roast it.' He continues ranting long enough to turn his wildlife kebab into a charred remain.

Noah takes the cook at his word and resists cheeking him further. He watches Sergeant Salt tuck into a cooked squirrel—a tree-rat kebab—served with chopped fur-tail garnish, while the privates and lance corporals have to make do with ground-rat kebabs with chopped bald-tail garnish.

The yellow-coated fellow wanders over to sit nearer the fire. The cook addresses him as Major Tom and hands him an enamel dish containing a meal of barbecued rabbit with scut garnish and diced carrots. At closer quarters, Noah realises the major bears a striking resemblance to the Saluki-girl in Kate's dressing room, with his sable-brown wavy hair and refined features.

Someone called Captain Mac joins the major. This black-haired fellow is dressed in a sky-blue jacket and has a large drawstring purse hung from his belt. It clinks and jingles as he walks. He eats his rabbit straight from the bayonet, no doubt to prove he is one of the lads.

Noah's stomach grumbles with a mixture of nerves and hunger. The rabbit smells good.

The last of the officers to appear is Lieutenant Stark, who wears a bright pink coat and matching peaked cap. His crazy antics offer a timely distraction to Noah. First, he beats his uncooked dinner—a pigeon—with his walking cane about fifty times to tenderise the meat. After this, he skewers the flattened pigeon with his sword. Holding the hilt of the sword with one paw-hand, he gives the pigeon a small turn over the flame every thirty seconds, measuring the seconds by beating the tip of his walking cane on a block of wood with his other paw-hand. Noah reckons mastering such a feat of co-ordination would drive even the sanest of characters mad.

One of the privates shoves a cooked whole rat through the bars of Bluebell's cage and saves the garnish for himself. Bluebell chews lazily on the offering without eating it, and then discards it all together. She lies down, chin on paws, and fixes Noah with a hang-puppy expression, as if to say *can we go home, now?* The tip of her tail wags in a doubting way.

Noah forces a reassuring smile for her benefit, without an idea in his head what to do about her plight. The longer they're away from home, the more the situation seems his fault and the harder it is to ignore the what-ifs. Yes, Kate did go shopping all day and leave Bluebell on her own, and, yes, she did own a ridiculous room full of shoes that had proved a chewing haven to a bored puppy. But he had been the one to shoot stagnant green muck in her eye with his water pistol, and he had been the one who went on the computer when he should have been in bed.

'Here, mutant, stop daydreaming and stuff this in your gob.' The cook slides a tail-less ground rat off his blade and chucks it at Noah.

The sizzling hot rodent glances off Noah's arm and lands on the ground on top of a battalion of ants. He raises his bound hands as a reminder. 'Gob? How?'

'Untie him. One hand only,' says Sergeant Salt to the private who fed Bluebell.

The private removes the rope from both wrists, straight away retying the left one twice as tight. Noah wriggles the fingers of his free hand and circles his wrist a few times to ease the cramp and get his blood circulating again. He stretches down to pick up the rat. It has a few scorched ants stuck to its barbecued back. Unable to brush the ants off, Noah tells himself they will add protein to his meal. It is important he sets Bluebell an example by showing her rats covered in ants are edible.

Noah bites into the rat's side and thinks of his schoolteacher, Mr Williams, raving on about French medieval history. Fancy ending up eating rats like the poor, starving, besieged citizens of Calais once did. If only he was a celebrity on reality TV, then at least he would get paid a million pounds for chomping through such a meal.

Having overcome his disgust at eating a creature associated with plague and death, he's surprised at how similar to chicken it tastes. It might have tasted even better, without the toothy head. To Noah's relief, Bluebell gives her meal a second chance, but his relief is short-lived as she starts to gag on fragments of splintery bone.

'Puppies aren't allowed cooked bones,' Noah tells the private who untied him. The fellow ignores him and carries on munching on his kebab. Noah tries again. 'She'll choke, if you don't take the bones away.'

He looks up at Noah, wipes his greasy jowl on the sleeve of his jacket, and lets out a loud belch. 'You talking to someone, mutant?'

'Yes.'

'Well, don't.'

In desperation, Noah calls out. 'Sergeant Salt, sir, please could you ask someone to remove that rat from my puppy?'

'Apart from the fact she ain't *your* puppy no more, I'll oblige your request, since you asked respectful, like.'

'Thank you, Sergeant Salt, sir.'

'Just guarding me interests, before you start thinking we're best mates, or somethink.'

Noah decides to leave the subject of property ownership where it is for the time being.

Sergeant Salt goes to the cage and extracts a huge bunch of keys from his pocket.

As he turns the key in the lock, Noah calls out to him again. 'Sergeant Salt, sir, could the puppy, whose name is Bluebell, have a drink of water, please?'

Salt wrinkles his snout in a warning snarl. 'Don't push it.'

'She'll die from thirst, sir.'

He squints at Noah, as if measuring the truth of his words, and then shouts at the private. 'Pegleg, get the puppy some water, and act sharp about it.'

Private Pegleg flings Noah a filthy look and goes to fetch some water from the lake in a tin cup. Noah notices he walks with a pronounced limp, so insulting nicknames are obviously the norm around here. He returns with the filled cup and hands it to Salt.

The sergeant inches the cage-door open and tries to extract the carcass from Bluebell's mouth. He offers her a drink in exchange, at the same time as using his elbow to stop the door opening further. Bluebell loosens her hold on the carcass and bites down on the sergeant's paw-hand with her needle-sharp milk teeth. With amazing self-control, Salt manages not to shout or drop the cup of water. But something has to give, and this something is the door.

A poo-smeared, squiggling, wiggling, semi-hysterical puppy lets go of the sergeant's paw-hand in favour of the cup, from which she takes a few hurried laps before tipping it over. She bounds out of the cage and starts jumping around Salt, barking, and wetting herself. Noah can see she is in one of her wind-ups, both cross and happy at the same time. Salt attempts to wrestle her to the ground, adding to the existing grubbiness of his uniform.

A couple of lance corporals sitting by the fire start sniggering at Salt: a foolish thing to do, Noah thinks, considering Salt has eyes in the back of his head.

'You lazy good-for-nothinks,' the sergeant shouts at them, 'get over here and do somethink about this hooligan of a mutt, before I lynch the pair of you.'

Bluebell continues to jump up and launch herself off him, using him as a springboard. But when the good-for-nothinks attempt to capture her, she loses interest in the sergeant and begins whizzing around in circles just out of their reach, with her tail down and her ears back so she looks more like a greyhound than a Labrador.

It is now Salt's turn to laugh.

One of the lance corporals lands flat on his face when Bluebell, without warning, decides to make a sharp departure from running circles to take a nose-dive under Noah's chair. Salt strides over and leans his wiry snout into Noah's face. 'This wild animal of yours, how do I tame it?'

Noah tells him straight. 'I don't own a wild animal, sir.'

'Quite right, mutant,' he says, showering Noah's

29

face with spittle. 'How then should I tame this wild animal in my custody?'

Noah notices Salt's three-cornered hat on the ground, dangerously close to Bluebell. Keen to strike up a deal fast, Noah says, 'Sir, you could appoint me as her handler, whilst you stayed in charge.'

Salt strokes his terrier-like whiskers with a paw-hand. 'If I was to do that, how exactly would it work?'

'Well, sir, you'd untie my feet and my other hand. Then you'd let me make a collar and lead out of the rope to keep Bluebell under control.'

Salt squints at Noah out of his dark, beady eyes. 'But how about the small point of keeping *you* under control?'

'It's like this, sir. This place is like an alien planet to me, and you're probably the least of its dangers. So it's better to take my chances staying with you, than running away.'

'Humph—seems good enough reasoning to me.'

'Does that mean you're going to untie me?' Noah fights to keep urgency from his voice, as Bluebell's eyes alight upon the hat.

'No.'

'No, sir?'

'Nope, it's Watt and Dittle's job, for having the cheek to laugh at me.' He makes the two lance corporals sound like a pair of notorious criminals, lawyers, or a bit of both.

Bluebell sniffs at the edge of Salt's hat in a hesitant way, doubtless with mixed feelings about its smell. This gives Noah a chance to buy further time and work out what to do about the additional problem.

'Oi, you good-for-nothinks,' Salt says to the lance corporals, 'me-self and mutant have reached a gentle-mong's agreement. Untie him. As I see it, he's not going anywhere fast.'

Freed, Noah throws himself down with a dramatic cry and plays dead. This brings Bluebell running at speed. As she climbs over him, licking his face, he grabs hold of her before she gets it into her mind to fetch Salt's hat for a game of tug-of-war.

<><><>

The vast meadow whiffs of over-rich grass that is dark, dense, and cool near its roots and sun-warmed at its tips. The light reflects off each blade, dazzling Noah. He has to blink extra fast to clear his watery eyes. For miles and miles in every direction there's nothing but neon green, dotted with wild flowers in vivid yellows, reds, oranges, and blues. Looking at it makes him feel queasy.

He and Graham Labrador take one handle each of an unzipped canvas holdall in which Bluebell rests, curled up after a long bout of leaping about amidst high grass on the end of her rope-lead, snapping at butterflies.

Noah's shoulders are killing him and he's starving. His last meal was breakfast, when Salt rewarded him for good behaviour with a raw skylark egg and a stick of fish. About an hour ago, Major Tom told Noah if he carried on behaving himself until supper, he would allow him and Bluebell a rabbit each.

Arriving at a dewpond, Noah copies everyone else and refills the flask Salt has given him. He's too thirsty to care if he picks up liver fluke from the water; this isn't a cosy school camping trip, but a march into the unknown. Bluebell sticks her nose in the dewpond a few times, laps up some water, sneezes, and then jumps about Noah, nipping at him harder than in normal play. Maybe this is her way of expressing mixed feelings about their situation.

They head towards a circle of standing stones that remind Noah of Stonehenge. The orange sun turns deep crimson and seems to liquefy across the far horizon as it sinks out of sight. The pink sun lingers for a while longer, before disappearing, too.

At the stones, a chill wind sweeps across the meadow, raising gooseflesh on Noah's arms. Bluebell appears intrigued by the whooshing, whispering sound of the wind in the grass. She sits there, very still, sniffing the air, with her ears blowing back, looking most regal and mature for someone so young. Noah feels honoured at catching a glimpse of who she'll become when grown-up. She reminds him of an oil painting of a gun dog. This peep into the future gives him hope.

Noah awakes to the rumble of thunder. In the watery sky, the diluted orange sun rests upon the horizon like a broken egg yolk floating in albumen. The pink sun is not due to rise yet, although Noah doubts it will get a look in, with all those dark-grey clouds tumbling in from the opposite horizon. They remind him of the malignancy that consumed his computer.

Clutching Bluebell close to him, he watches the clouds with a mixture of disquiet and vain hope they will suddenly move into reverse and land him and Bluebell back home.

Lightning cuts mauve-white zigzags in the clouds: a forward-march, relentless as a massed army of monsters with flashing swords. One of the swords reaches down and strikes a lone tree, splitting it in two and exploding it into flames. Noah seeks shelter behind one of the standing stones and prays for rain. He remembers what his dad told him about dry lightning: how extra dangerous it is, with no rain to put out the sparks.

'You feeling okay, Noah?' asks Graham, plonking himself down in the grass next to him.

'Huh? Yes. No,' he replies, thinking it a daft question, considering his and Bluebell's situation. It makes him wonder whose side Graham is on, if any. The Labrador-man doesn't appear to be a prisoner of the Lurchers anymore.

'You play your cards right, son, and you might get to stay with young four-leg.'

'Why? Is this some kind of game?' Noah thinks of the card game Cheat.

Graham appears to read his mind. 'If you try cheating on them, there's no turning them around to your way of thinking, ever. Show them the respect accorded to a real army. It could prove to your advantage further down the line. You might find any loyalty towards their present employer ends with payment for the job.'

'Their present employer being Percival, you mean?'

Graham visibly starts at mention of the name. 'Where did you hear that?'

'When I was lying on my back tied up, pretending to be unconscious.'

'Wish you hadn't.'

'Why?'

'Percival is very bad news.'

'Is he evil?'

'It depends where you draw a line between madness and evil.'

Their conversation fizzles out, as a huge raindrop plops down from the sky and bounces off Noah's nose. More drops start to fall all around, at first separate and lazy, but soon turned to vertical rods as ferocious as spears. As the storm moves closer, the clouds draw a

33

hood over the meadow. Wild gusts of wind swirl the rain around, transforming it into a spray of such density, Noah can see little beyond his immediate surroundings. At least he need not fear dry lightning frying him, but this still leaves him about twenty thousand terrifying things more to deal with.

Since arriving in this alternative reality of a world, which is his only explanation for the total weirdness of everything around him, Noah has fought to keep a handle on his emotions for the sake of his and Bluebell's survival. But now it's as if someone has kicked that door down and let out all those pent-up feelings at once. His legs, chafed pink by the deluge, turn wobbly as a chilled blancmange. Cold to the core, he hugs Bluebell close. Tears stream down his frozen cheeks and snot runs from his nose into his mouth. Full of love and concern, Bluebell licks his face.

An overhead thunderclap sounds, accompanied by a dazzling blue-white flash. A scream lodges, sharp, in Noah's throat. He squeezes his eyes tight shut. Bluebell lets out a low growl and a single deep bark, followed by higher pitched frantic barking. Despite her rain-drenched coat, Noah can feel her bristles stand erect in a ridge down her back, but fear has stitched his eyes together and he can't bring himself to open them.

Someone wrenches her from his arms and forces a wad of folded cloth over his face. The cloth covers his nose and mouth, forcing him to breathe in its sickly sweet smell. He flails about in an attempt to break free, but his limbs are about as useless as sails on a broken windmill.

Bluebell's desperate barks die away into the distance, until the thick rain swallows them up.

The sickly sweet smell forces a feeling of false

happiness upon Noah, even though he's wretched to the point of death. Then sleep blankets out his senses.

— CHAPTER FOUR —

Mad Psychiatrists and an Obsession with White

This is becoming a habit, thinks Noah, recovering consciousness to find himself imprisoned flat on his back. He's in a white room, which contrasts starkly with the black typhoon raging in his head. Bluebell has gone, he knows not where.

He thinks of a picture he once saw of an all-white heaven. What a joke. This place is an all-white hell: the bed (its frame and covers), the cupboard next to the bed, the walls, the ceiling, the light fixture, the bars on the windows, the paintwork, the door, the hand-restraints, and the one-piece shell suit swathed about him. White, white, white. Doubtless the floor is white, too.

With every beat of his heart, his yearning grows for home, or rather for random things to do with his city. The sound of seagulls, swishing waves, and a gale-force wind whipping flags about poles; the smell and taste of salt; slimy green rock-pools full of crabs; old shells; vinegary fish and chips wrapped in paper and eaten out in the fresh air; hot pavements; shimmering roads;

cycling through traffic jams; the stink of petrol and diesel fumes locked in a heat haze: anything other than this sterile whiteness and deep silence, broken on and off by muffled dog barks.

<><><><>

He awakens to voices in the room but pretends to stay asleep.

'How's your other half doing, these days?' says a male voice.

A female replies. 'You know how it is. Private medicine's booming. Jason only does a couple of clinics a week now. The rest of the time he gets to play golf.'

'No more research, then?'

'His health started to suffer, what with all the to-ing and fro-ing he did.'

'Doesn't seem to have hurt him in the long-term, though.'

'Only time will tell.'

'No signs of premature ageing, then?'

'Not that I can see … maybe a little more forgetful than he used to be.'

'Still, this latest case is most interesting, thanks to Jason and his associates. Do remember me to him … Perhaps a spot of sailing sometime, followed by a dinner at the yacht club?'

'Am I included in the invitation?'

This last question provokes a marked clearing of the throat from the male, followed by a few moments of hesitation. 'But you're female, and—'

'And a *mere* nurse.'

'That wasn't what I was going to say—not at all, Sister Cairn, not at all.'

'Well, Dr Borzoi, I'm very glad to hear it—very glad indeed.'

Noah's eyes snap open before he can stop them. Curiosity killed the boy, he thinks.

Dr Borzoi lets out a forever Ah sound; the sort of Ah that only medics or vicars do. It goes something like *Ahrrrrrrrrrrrrrrrrrrrrrrrrrahrrrrrrrrrrrrrrrrrrrrrrrrrahrrroh.* The exclamation seems to travel up the windpipe of his elongated neck before he uncloses his mouth a crack to let it escape. The nose at the end of his long, slim aristocratic snout is only centimetres from Noah's face. His breath smells of spearmint mouthwash.

'And how are you feeling, Master Padgett?' he asks.

'Oi, how do you know my surname, Dr Borzoi?'

'Oh, I know a lot about you, thanks to Sister Cairn-here's husband. Yes, thank you very much. Thank you very much indeed. You like to be called Noah, don't you?'

'Not by strangers, no. It's none of your business what my name is.'

'Sparky, isn't he, Sister? Most sparky, if I might say so, but we won't write it in his notes just yet. Perhaps I should call him by his hospital number instead.'

Sister Cairn refers to the cover of the white file she has in her paw-hands. 'That will be patient number six-thousand two-hundred and twenty-three, Doctor.'

'Sounds a good-enough number to me.'

'It's a silly number,' says Noah, dismissing Borzoi as a nutcase. He longs to find out what has happened to Bluebell, but his instincts tell him to bide his time.

The doctor stands there looking thoughtful, pinching the end of his snout between his dewclaw and one of his digital pads. 'I've got it!' He waggles the equivalent of an index finger at Noah. 'Your name can be Haon.'

'That's pathetic, Dr Iozrob.'

38

'Indeed, indeed, indeed, Haon—twenty out of ten for passing the word-reversal test. I note you are someone who doesn't allow emotions to cloud your intellect. I think Sister Cairn can safely remove your restraints.'

Taking a bunch of keys from her pocket, Sister unlocks the white handcuffs. Noah gives his wrists and back a rub, stretches a bit, and sits up on the edge of the bed. He notices the floor has a thick pile white carpet, identical to the one Kate had in her dressing room before Bluebell soiled it with wee.

By the time he leaves off staring at the carpet, he realises the doctor and the nurse have slipped from the room and shut the door behind them. He never heard them go, padding softly on their thin-soled shoes. For a moment he allows himself to believe they might have forgotten to secure the door, as he can't see a handle or lock on the inside.

He walks across the room in his bare feet, aware of the carpet squeezing its dense fibres up between his toes: fat, hairy caterpillars. He tests the door, first with a gentle push and then by putting his full weight into it, but it won't budge. Fighting the desire to scream and kick the door, he sits down cross-legged on the floor to contemplate his situation.

In his world, some people have found themselves imprisoned illegally for years, if not for the rest of their lives. Champions for their release would call it a 'human rights issue', but what about here? Why would they bother with human rights?

'I'm doomed,' he says, clutching at his head in despair. Nobody back home, including the British Government, the security services, or human rights' lawyers, have heard of Dr Stefano Borzoi.

39

<><><>

He has a visitor.

Sybil Spaniel is smelly and overweight, with tan and white fur and freckles. She wears a pinafore top, frumpy floral skirt, and ankle socks with lace-up shoes. 'This place is Roomdaorb Hospital for the Criminally Insane and I'm a patient here,' she says, by means of an introduction.

'Why are you a patient?' Noah asks.

'The reason changes every month, depending on Dr Borzoi's mood. This month, he has rewarded me for my good behaviour by appointing me as Master Padgett's personal attendant and companion.'

'What does the doctor see as good behaviour?'

'Almost anything *un*dog-like.'

'But he's a dog himself, so how can he talk?'

'Is he?'

'Sort of.'

'If he hears you calling him a dog, he'll stop treating you as an honoured guest.'

'Hardly the way to treat an honoured guest, locking him up in a white room without explanation.'

Sybil thrusts a tray at Noah, avoiding eye contact. 'Are you going to eat your breakfast?'

'What? Puffed wheat and carrot? Not likely.' Noah has a sore throat, headache, and queasy stomach from whatever noxious substance knocked him out. Sea-salted hand-baked potato crisps are the only thing he fancies.

'Don't let Dr Borzoi hear you saying "no" to food, either.'

'Why, is he Big Brother?'

Sybil stands there looking nonplussed, as if someone has temporarily thrown the off-switch in her head.

40

'Oh, never mind. Tell me one good reason why I should eat it.'

'Cos if you don't, Dr Borzoi will want to check if you're ill. That means blood tests, x-rays, throat spatulas, gastric tubes, brain scans, spine—'

Noah holds up his hand. 'Stop! Message received, loud and clear.'

He chomps his way through the dry and unappetising breakfast, working hard to convince himself it's a better option than someone force-feeding him prunes, kippers, lumpy semolina, or sour rhubarb. When he has finished eating, he asks Sybil if he can go to the bathroom.

'To do what?' she asks.

'Well, you know ... the usual.'

'No, I don't know.'

'Must I spell it out?'

She wrinkles her snout and sniggers into her paw. 'Only joking.'

Noah prefers the switched-off version of Sybil. There's something very unnerving about a criminally insane spaniel dressed like an overgrown primary school girl. She could have a very, very, very warped sense of humour.

Noah jiggles about a bit, to make his point. 'Quick! The bathroom, this minute, or else...'

'Dr Borzoi will be pleased.'

'About what? I don't care what Dr Borzoi thinks or what pleases him.'

'Best if you do.'

Sybil crosses the room and places one of her paw-hands a little above centre of the door, which opens with ease. This infuriates Noah, considering all his efforts and deliberations of earlier. Perhaps Sybil is microchipped, so she can let herself in and out of rooms in the same way some chipped cats let themselves in and out of houses through posh little electronic cat-ports.

Noah goes with Sybil from the white room. They walk along one lengthy white corridor after another, passing several dog-men and dog-women of different breeds or crossbreeds, dressed in unisex blue and pink striped boiler suits. The colours they're wearing help break the white monotony. All of them are on cleaning duty, scrubbing the already spotless floors, washing the already spotless walls, polishing the already spotless windows, and wiping down the vertical security bars in front of these windows.

Outside the door with the word TELIOT written on it, Noah mutters under his breath, 'Of course, we're in the land of not very clever letter reversals.'

'What are you talking about?' asks Sybil.

'Nothing in particular.' He changes the subject abruptly, hoping to short her out, so he can turn his mind to escaping. 'What species are you?'

She remains alert. 'We're *Canis sapiens*, of course. Don't you know anything?'

'Not a lot.' Noah adopts a loose-mouthed, blank-eyed expression for her benefit. 'I need to go to the toilet now, if you don't mind.'

She starts to follow him.

'On my own,' he adds.

She cocks her head on one side. 'Why?'

''Cause you're a girl.'

'Yako.'

'Okay. Thanks.'

'You'll find the moor-htab adjoined to the teliot.'

'Yako,' says Noah, giving his armpits a sniff. 'Is that an unsubtle hint?'

He finds the seat to the teliot pan most interesting. Unlike Graham's very basic outdoor loo, it has a gap at the back to accommodate a dog-person's tail: not that Noah has seen so much as a bulge in the back of any of their clothing so far, so they must keep their tails well hidden.

To the right of the teliot pan is a dispenser with moist bottom wipes. On the wall, above this, a choice of twelve different sized five-pad flushers to depress. Noah sticks the end of his forefinger in the Chihuahua-sized one.

The moor-htab beyond, has white tiling throughout and an unremarkable white washbasin, bath, shower, and a pile of coarse-looking folded up white towels stacked on a white stool screwed firmly to a white linoleum floor.

In a cupboard above the washbasin, Noah finds a variety of doggy-delights: non-foaming toothpaste, mouthwash that smells of disinfectant, moisturising balm for a dry nose, softening emollient for paw-pads, eye wipes, and ear wipes. A plastic notice affixed to the wall reads…

USE OF RAZORS, SCISSORS, AND NAIL-CLIPPERS STRICTLY UNDER SUPERVISION OF NURSING STAFF

Before going to the toilet or taking a shower, Noah checks the area for hidden cameras or places where periscopes might surface. Everything seems in order, although he worries about what spying gadget might lurk in the showerhead.

Even at the hottest setting, the water is tepid. He washes all over with the non-foaming dog shampoo, which has a more acceptable smell than the mouthwash.

It reminds him of the lemon balm in his garden back home.

The moment he picks up the towel, there's a knock at the teliot door. The timing of this seems too much of a coincidence to dismiss. The possibility of hidden cameras enters his mind once more.

He calls out. 'Who is it?'

'Only Sybil. I've got some clean clothes for you.'

He wraps the towel around him and fetches a bundle from her. It consists of a baggy sky-blue T-shirt, navy-blue tracksuit bottoms, and extra-large slipper-socks that Sybil says Ulric St Bernard wore during his stay here.

Dr Hubert Bloodhound and Staff Nurse Susan Collie oversee a group therapy session for Noah and six other new patients. They sit in a semicircle, doctor and nurse included.

Dr Bloodhound peers over his half-moon spectacles at them. 'I would like each of you to introduce yourself by name and then explain, in a sentence or two, why you think you're in Roomdaorb Hospital. Perhaps, Miss Jack Russell, you would like to go first.'

The dog-girl has a white face, apart from a brown patch surrounding her left eye and covering one ear. It gives her the appearance of being two personalities rolled into one. 'Me? Oh, okay, if I must. My name is Minnie. I'm here because I bunked off work and spent my days down rabbit holes chasing the blighters.'

Before he can stop himself, Noah blurts out, 'But that's what Jack Russells do.'

Dr Bloodhound leans forward and shakes his floppy jowls at him, releasing a streamer of spittle from his mouth. 'It is most certainly *not* what Jack Russells do, and I would appreciate you keeping your opinions to yourself and waiting your turn, thank you. Next please...'

'My name is Bonzo,' says a Bulldog-man, gathering up his wrinkles into a dense frown. 'I kept digging up the flower beds and making holes in the grass in Notserp Park.'

'And?' asks Staff Nurse Collie.

Bonzo scratches at his fat cheek and looks up at the ceiling. 'I did it with my front-paws while down on all fours.'

The doctor reminds him, 'Not front-paws, Mister Bulldog. Top-paws, if you please.'

'Blooming load of nonsense, this is,' says the next patient, who has a broad forehead and wide-apart eyes filled with disdain.

'Mrs Beagle,' says Dr Bloodhound, 'I have already told Master Padgett to desist from expressing his opinions, and the same goes for everyone else here. Now say what you are meant to say, and go no further.'

'Certainly, doctor, if you insist. I am Tamara, whose greatest delight is to roll in fox's scat—a pastime not appreciated by my ex-husband, who reported me to the Master of the Hunt, who then reported me to the High Commissioner of Police.'

'Your greatest delight *was* to roll in scat, in the past-tense, not *is*,' the staff nurse reminds her.

'Next,' says Dr Bloodhound, to a Labrador-youth whose coat is more orange than yellow, indicating the possibility of some crossbreeding somewhere in his family tree.

'The name's Phil. And I say it's too bad Notserp Park's gotten taken over by the snoop-brigade. They lurk about in the bushes spying on us and looking for excuses

45

to dob us in to the so-called authorities.'

The doctor fixes Phil with a no-nonsense look. 'If you don't mind—'

'I do mind very much. It's an infringement of civil liberties. The park is for recreational purposes, including a bit of rough and tumble.'

Dr Bloodhound leans forward in his chair, the folds of his forehead falling forward in a grave manner. 'But it is *not* for playing chase down on all fours and rolling about, biting your playmates.'

'Harrumph.' Phil crosses his arms over his chest and gives Dr Bloodhound the hairy eyeball.

The doctor writes a long paragraph in a note pad with a scratchy pen. He ends by gouging and stabbing the paper with an underlining followed by a full stop. It seems as if some very unpleasant fate awaits the spirited Phil, which Noah thinks is a shame, as he'd like to have a chance of hanging out with him a bit.

'Lord MacScottish Terrier, if you please,' says Dr Bloodhound.

A dog-man of more senior years, with shaggy dark eyebrows, squared-off grey whiskers, and stained teeth, growls at the doctor.

Dr Bloodhound scribbles again, this time on a prescription pad. He tears off a sheet and hands it to Staff Nurse Collie. 'Make sure to deliver this to the pharmacy by 36.00 hours ZDT.' To the growling patient, he says, 'We won't put up with that type of aggression at Roomdaorb. Behave yourself, or I shall drop Mac and Lord from your name.'

Lord MacScottish shows his teeth again. 'You dare, and I'll bite the seat out of your trousers.'

'Which is,' says the doctor, 'precisely the kind of behaviour for which you were sent here in the first place.'

'What do you expect when the post-hound only delivers bills and tax demands? It is an unadulterated cheek to expect a fellow of my good breeding—Lord Hamish MacScottish Terrier of Hgrubnide who has served the kingdom through two great wars—to be harangued from pillar to post by bean counters.'

Dr Bloodhound taps his pen on his notepad, while taking a few deep breaths. In a measured tone, laced with sarcasm, he says, 'With respect, Mr Scottish Terrier, none of this is the post-hound's concern. He is just doing his job and does not expect to find himself pinned up against the gate, having his trousers ripped off him every time he delivers a brown envelope to your door. If ever you are to return home, it will be necessary to have someone install a letterbox outside the main gates to your property, should you suffer any relapse in behaviour.'

'Phooey.' Lord Hamish sticks out his unhealthy-looking bluish-yellow tongue at the doctor.

Dr Bloodhound glances up at a wall-clock: a very strange clock indeed, thinks Noah. It gives the illusion of being completely square, even though its horizontals have ten numbers each and its verticals eleven. The numbers start with '1' in the top right-hand corner, moving anticlockwise round to '38'. Noah reckons, for it to work, the corner numbers must represent a longer span of time than the other numbers on the clock's face. As he sits there puzzling over whether the numbering has something to do with the twin suns, he becomes aware of Dr Bloodhound watching him.

The doctor clears his throat to get his full attention. 'Uh, hum, right. Now Master Padgett is back with us, he can hear what Miss Golden Retriever has to say.'

She fiddles with a lock of her ear-hair and looks down at her lap. 'My name's Suzie, but me mates call me Goldie. I like eating poo—especially me own.'

'Yum, tasty,' says Phil Labrador with a snigger.

Dr Bloodhound ignores him and glances up at the clock once more. 'I'm very much aware of the time, and we don't want to miss the opportunity of hearing from young Master Padgett.'

Noah is desperate to avoid one of Dr Bloodhound's prescriptions, so plays safe. 'I'd be most grateful if you spoke for me—please, sir.'

The doctor motions towards him with his paw-hand. 'No, you go first. Do give us the benefit of your opinion.'

Noah decides not to mention Bluebell, on the grounds the medic is playing with him the same as Dr Borzoi had done the day before. 'I think it's because I'm a newly-discovered species and you want to study me.'

The doctor brings his paw-hands together in a slow clap-clapping motion. 'Correct first time, Master Padgett. Well done. I declare our first therapy session closed for lunch. Same time, same place, next week.'

CHAPTER FIVE

Card Games with the Resistance Party

O ver what feels like the Earth-equivalent of two months, Noah has compiled a list of all the obstacles to his escaping Roomdaorb Hospital. For the umpteenth time, he gets out his folded up scrap of paper from its hiding place under a loose tile in the bathroom. Perhaps today, if he studies the list hard enough, it will reveal a way out. He reads and considers each item in turn.

1. *There are heavy iron bars in front of all the windows (*no cutting tools available*).*
2. *The windows are locked (*no keys available*).*
3. *The outer doors are controlled by electronic devices needing Level One clearance identity microchips to operate them (*no chipped friends, apart from Sybil Spaniel, who's Level Four. No help*).*
4. *All members of the nursing staff are armed with stun guns (*speaks for itself*).*

5. *The corridors are patrolled by armed security guards with the surname Dobermann Pinscher (*revolvers kill*).*

6. *Throughout the hospital there are loads of tiny security cameras that keep being moved about (*can't map out a definite escape route*).*

7. *All the daylight hours—averaging 26—are filled with patients doing pointless repetitive tasks (*leaves 12 hours of darkness—8 in bed*).*

8. *Outdoor recreation forbidden (*nowhere outside to go, apart from the roof & a sheer drop to the water*).*

9. *The hospital is on an island in the middle of a 400 square kilometre freshwater lake. Neither the lake nor the island were there before the giant, Finn McDrool Irish Wolfhound, lost his temper and carved up the landscape with his gigantic paws (*my water phobia, but I like the sound of a hairy giant*).*

10. *Finn McDrool Irish Wolfhound is a legend, or is he? (*how I wish*).*

11. *It's rumoured that piranha fish populate the lake and can strip* Canis sapiens *down to their skeletons in minutes. No one has lived to confirm this (*gross*).*

12. *Supplies airlifted in and dropped from a height on to the flat roof (*Level One clearance required. See 8*).*

13. *~~It's considered unlucky to try escaping~~ (silly comment that's asking for trouble—delete this item).*

<><><>

Overnight, as always, a complete shift change of staff appears to have taken place, although it's hard for Noah to tell if this includes the security guards, as they all look the same to him.

Only a second or two after he has returned his list to his hiding place, Sybil Spaniel comes into his room and says to him, 'If you're thinking about escaping, forget it. There's no landing pad for a helicopter, no aircraft strip, and nowhere to tie up a boat.'

Noah feels his cheeks reddening. 'I've no idea what you're talking about,' he says rather too quickly, wondering if she has read his list and is a spy for Dr Borzoi.

She does her usual sniggering into her paw-hand, 'Only teasing. You look so guilty, that's all.'

'Oh, well. If you'll excuse me, I'm just off to hang out with my friends.' He hurries out of his room, at a speed faster than Sybil's slippers will take her, and heads for the communal day room without looking back. It's his once-fortnightly day off from repetitive tasks and he has arranged to meet up with the six dog-people who share group-therapy sessions with him and have become his friends.

When he arrives there, he finds the others have invited along Dorothy Dalmatian, who's attractive looking; she has a sleek white head dotted with black spots the size of coins. She goes all shy around Noah, although, according to the others, this is unusual, as her reason for being in the hospital is for the crime of bouncing around strangers and barking with excitement.

He asks her, 'What's criminally insane about being over-energetic?'

51

She shakes her head.

Phil answers for her. 'You heard what old Doc "droopy-eyes" Bloodhound has to say about each of us. We're breaking the law.'

'So why not just prosecute you? You're hardly hurting anyone badly enough to justify them locking you up in a nuthouse.'

'I *did* bite the post-hound,' Hamish MacScottish Terrier reminds Noah.

'You could wear a muzzle.'

'What's a muzzle?' asks Bonzo Bulldog.

'Not something you could wear with...' (Noah just stops himself in time from commenting on Bonzo's undershot jaw and flat face) '...your habit of digging.'

Bonzo frowns, multiplying his wrinkles. 'What's it got to do with digging?'

'Well, presumably you're digging for *something* when you dig, which means leaving your mouth free to retrieve whatever it is?'

'Can't say I've ever dug for anything other than digging's sake. On the other paw-hand, it sounds quite exciting digging for something rather than nothing. Think I might try it. What do you suggest?'

'If I didn't think it would get you into even more trouble, I'd suggest meat bones or rubber toys. But you need a decent patch of mud or grass first, which is in rather short supply inside this building.'

'Now *that* is where you are wrong,' says Bonzo. 'There's Horticulture.'

A tiny flame of optimism flickers to life in Noah. 'Why's no-one mentioned that before?'

Tamara Beagle seems to catch on to where his thoughts are leading. 'Horticulture is gardening. Gardening needs mud. Mud means out-of-doors.'

'You could have pretend out-of-doors, with pretend sunshine and pretend rain,' says Dorothy Dalmatian.

Bonzo puffs out his chest and looks rather pleased at having got everyone's attention. 'Apparently, some patients from the Rehabilitation Unit go to Horticulture to learn about growing fruit and vegetables. It's meant to help them get a job after leaving here.'

'Jolly good bit of underground work, old fellow,' says Lord Hamish MacScottish Terrier, 'most impressive, if I say so myself. Who've you been talking to, Bonzo?'

'The skinny Jimmy Whippet, who claims to be so fast that he gets to see things before others see him. This doesn't yet include sussing out the exits from this place. You won't be surprised to hear he's addicted to stealing, especially food, even when he isn't hungry. The not-so-good news is that, despite his many skills, he's been in here for four years without making it outside the building.'

This last piece of information casts a renewed sense of hopelessness over Noah. He may be here forever, or at least until he's an old man of his dad's age, by which time Bluebell will be long dead, if she isn't already.

Tamara Beagle asks, 'Did Jimmy Whippet happen to mention if there's anything nice and smelly to roll in down at Rehab?'

Lord Hamish glowers at her from under his shaggy eyebrows. 'For Cosmo's sake!'

'Wonder if there're any rabbits there,' says Minnie Jack Russell.

Phil Labrador points a paw-hand at his own head. 'Duh! Why'd anybody with even half a brain, allow a load of flipping bunnies near carrots and lettuce?'

Tamara chuckles to herself.

Phil says, 'Look, I'm serious, okay.'

'Think about it, Philip—'

'Nobody *Philips* me. I'm Phil, right.'

Tamara throws him a winning smile. 'I just wanted to say, Phil, that when we speak of the quarter-brains who govern this place, we are dealing with a wagonload of dogs who believe they are something other than dogs. So tell me, who are the deluded ones, them or us?'

'I get your point,' says Phil.

'Which means, those who consider themselves in charge around here might indeed let a "load of flipping bunnies" loose near carrots and lettuce.'

Suzie 'Goldie' Golden Retriever sits there, twiddling a lock of ear-hair around her paw as usual. Noah asks her if she has anything to contribute to the discussion about Horticulture.

'You can count me in, if you're planning an undercover visit to Horticulture that might involve rabbits,' she says.

Minnie points a claw at her. 'Oi, I'm the one who gets to eat the rabbits, not you.'

'Who said anything about eating the rabbit?' says Goldie. 'It's their scrummy poos I'm interested in.'

Noah has noticed something interesting about Goldie. She doesn't act as common around her friends as she does around the doctors or nursing staff. It's as if she works harder to hide something from those qualified to see through her.

Bonzo asks her, 'Would you like me to root out a few pineapple suckers and kill the blighters while we're at it?'

To Noah this seems an innocent enough question, although maybe slightly wacky. But Goldie claps her paw-hands to her ears and emits a sound that is a cross-between barking and wailing, indicating the question is far from innocent.

Phil stands up and looms over Bonzo, shaking his fist at him. 'Why'd you have to go and spoil things by saying *that* word?'

Noah asks, 'What word?'

'Blooming pineapples,' blurts out Tamara.

Goldie disappears under the nearest chair and stays there, quivering.

Noah mutters in Tamara's ear. 'What's the problem with unmentionable whatsits?'

'They crush them up and keep adding them to her food, so her poos taste foul.'

'What? All of her meals?'

'Yes, all of them.'

'Well that's a bit rough. Couldn't they wean her off the habit, little by little?'

'Apparently it never works doing it that way. One taste of poo and she'll go on a total binge, stuffing her face with it until she's fit to burst.'

One of the nursing staff—an overweight black and tan coloured Cavalier King Charles Spaniel-man, whose name Noah doesn't know—glances over at them but is too lazy to shift himself from his seat.

Noah kneels down next to Golden Retriever-girl and strokes all around her ears, neck, and chin to soothe her. She relaxes to his touch, as would Bluebell, who is never far from his thoughts. An intense feeling of wretchedness hits him without warning. His face crumples and a stray tear trickles from his eye. He dabs the tear away, blinks fast, and stifles a sniff.

'Sorry for making you sad,' says Goldie.

Her kind voice makes Noah even sadder. She reminds him of how his mum, Shelley, used to be—

55

afraid of life, yet always caring towards others: a rough Peckham girl with a soft centre. This makes him want to cry even more. 'No, it's not you. I'm just thinking about my puppy, Bluebell, and wondering if she's being treated kindly.' He does not mention his mum. The pain of losing her is something he keeps to himself, as he hates anyone telling him how he should feel.

Goldie smiles at him out of her glistening dark-cocoa eyes. We'll find Bluebell for you.'

'How?'

'My papa's favourite saying is "intention buys direction". Perhaps the two of us should put it into action, as I'm sick of being force-fed prickly-skinned tropical fruit and you're sick of not having your puppy, and we both want to get out of here.'

Bloated from eating too much rabbit stew, carrots, and corn-dumplings for lunch (plus all the crushed pineapple sneaked off Goldie's plate), Noah returns to the day room and flops out in front of the box-shaped four-screen telly with his friends.

There's only one screen switched on just now. Their overweight attendant of earlier—a Nursing Assistant who goes under the name of Charlie—is watching a quiz show.

The contestants are Shane Mongrel, Wayne Mongrel, Tracy Yorkshire Terrier (complete with pink bow and straightened hair), Kevin Bull Terrier, and Sharon Miniature Poodle (of the oversize hoop earrings and face glitter). The quizmaster—Breagan Rottweiler—asks them questions, such as, which is the largest: a mouse or an elephant? Do chickens give birth to live chicks or lay eggs? Does pork come from a cow, a goose, a pig, or a horse? Does a hermit live in a town centre, a commune, a hotel, or a cave?

Charlie answers the first couple of questions before the contestants, but then finds himself outdone by Wayne Mongrel and Sharon Miniature Poodle for the next two.

Lord Hamish registers his disgust at the programme with a grunt and a scowl.

Bonzo picks up a magazine and bangs it down hard on the coffee table next to him. 'If I'm forced to endure one minute more of this un-stimulating rubbish, it'll kill off every brain cell in my head.'

Phil laughs. 'If that's all it takes, you can't have many brain cells in the first place.'

Bonzo rolls up the magazine and swipes Phil on the leg with it. 'That's a darned cheek coming from a dumbhead like you.'

'Well, you want to know what I think?' says Tamara. 'Sharon Miniature Poodle is wearing far too much mascara.'

Charlie yells across at them. 'How, in Zyx's name, am I meant to concentrate with you lot making all that noise? Just shut-the-*findledock* up.'

Hamish grunts again.

'How about a game of cards?' asks Goldie, who is in a much better mood after her pineapple-free lunch.

'Only if it's possible for Minnie Jack Russell to keep her temper,' says Bonzo. 'She's always such a bad loser.'

Goldie draws two packs of cards out of a concealed side-pocket in her striped boiler suit. She tips them out of their packets and does a fancy card shuffle. This involves placing her two metacarpal pads on a nearby table and doing a manoeuvre called the double-fan dewclaw whizz. Watching her, Noah almost wishes he had pads and dewclaws rather than standard-issue human hands.

They pull some chairs up to the table. Goldie deals out seven cards each for seven players and five leftovers placed face-down in a discard pile.

'What do you call this game?' asks Noah.

'Taurus-plop,' says Tamara.

'Interesting name.' He picks up his card hand—a mix of clubs, spades, and hearts, with the king-of-hearts a St Bernard dog-man wearing a crown.

'I'll go first,' says Lord Hamish MacScottish Terrier.

'Isn't anybody going to explain the rules to me before we start?' Noah asks.

'No,' says Bonzo Bulldog. 'You already know the game. It's universal.'

'Okay.'

Lord Hamish places a couple of cards face-down on the table. 'Two aces.'

From his left, Tamara Beagle puts five cards on top of his. 'A two, two threes, a four, and a five.'

Bonzo gives her a sideways look. 'Hum.'

Phil adds a further few to the number. 'Three sixes, three sevens, two eights, and one nine.' He yawns and closes his eyes, as if he's about to fall asleep

Everyone shouts in unison. 'Taurus-plop!'

Phil's unsuccessful bluff earns him every card in the pile.

Noah recognises the game now, mostly from the noise. It's Cheat.

Charlie yells across at them again. 'Shut it, will you? It's time for kick-off.'

Tamara mutters, 'I just cannot see the point of anyone flopping in a chair to watch a load of overpaid *Canis sapiens* charging around a pitch after a leather ball.'

'Cut the fella some slack,' says Phil Labrador. 'I

enjoy sitting on my backside fighting trolls and dragons on my Z-box. It doesn't mean I'm looking to get my monster-slaying abilities up to scratch for a real life play-off. What's the difference?'

Noah is just about to compare the various merits of his X-box with Phil's Z-box, when the ref's whistle sounds and he finds himself transfixed by the surreal sight of *Canis sapiens* rushing around a football pitch, the players made up of a mix of mongrel, collie, terrier, whippet, and lurcher dog-men. One team has red-striped shirts and plain red shorts. The other team has plain purple shirts and purple-striped shorts. The ref is a French Bulldog-man dressed in black.

Amongst the supporters of the purple team, there's an abundance of pit-bull terrier-youths with diamond-shaped emblems shaved in the middle of their foreheads. When things are going well for their team, they thrust their paw-fists in the air and yell 'Lambast City', but when things are going badly, they snarl and head-butt the red team's fans from Yarridge West.

Phil elbows Noah and points to his card-hand. 'It's your turn.'

'No, it's not. It's yours,' Noah says. 'You just cheated.'

Phil smirks as he places some more cards face down on the table. 'Two tens, two jacks, two queens, and one king.'

Noah shouts 'Cheat' and the others shout 'Taurus-plop'.

Phil uncovers the cards. This time he tells the truth.

'We all challenged him at once, so who has the cards?' asks Noah.

'You, of course, as you called out the wrong word,' says Goldie.

He picks up the cards. 'Fiddlesticks.'

By the time the ref's whistle on the telly blows for half time, the card-game has not progressed any further, as nobody is much good at doing a successful bluff.

Charlie waddles over to them and holds out a plump paw-hand. 'I'll have those cards. I'm not putting up with you spoiling the second half of the match with your shouting.'

'No way,' says Phil, spread-eagling himself over the table on top of the cards.

'You want to go to the Clinic?' asks Charlie.

'You don't scare me that easily. Anyway the Clinic is closed at weekends.'

'I can easily get it opened.'

'If you do that, you'll miss the rest of the match, not to mention the senior member of staff who'll have to leave the footie to stick a needle in my backside.'

Charlie backs off. 'Okay, but just button it up, would you?'

'To tell the truth,' says Tamara, 'I am getting bored with playing Taurus-plop. Let's play Tiger and Vole instead.'

Golden Retriever girl starts to explain the rules, which sound like a variant on Spite and Malice, but three-quarters of the way through her explanation, Noah ceases to listen. On-screen, the camera has just panned across a section of lager-swigging fans and zoomed in on what the commentator calls 'First Class'. This is a special viewing gallery, complete with armed Staffordshire bull terrier bodyguards in black jumpsuits and black sunglasses.

Semi-reclining on a chaise longue with his arm draped along the short armrest is a large white poodle-man dressed in an expensive-looking emerald-green velvet suit. He sips from a champagne glass, with one of his claws held up like a pinkie. Next to him on the open end of this long couch, a chocolate Labrador puppy wearing an emerald-green velvet collar sits chewing on a soft toy.

Noah leaps up out of his chair so fast, he almost blacks out. 'That's my puppy ... look ... my puppy ... everybody look!' His shouted words echo in his head, and seem to belong to someone else.

Her snout is longer than the last time he saw her, her coat denser, the base of her tail thicker, and her eyes more yellow, but it's still his Bluebell.

His heart beats fast as a runaway train on the point of de-railing, powered by a combination of terror and joy. She's there and yet out of reach, looking relaxed amidst strange company, and not pining for him one little bit. It's a relief to see her captors treating her well, but Noah's jealousy of them and his desperation to reclaim Bluebell amounts to agony.

'Hey Noah, you want a trip to the Clinic, too?' asks Nursing Assistant Charlie.

'But that puppy belongs to me, not to that idiotic-looking poodle,' shouts Noah.

'You don't want to let any of the security guards around here hear you saying that. They're probably best buddies with Percival's heavies.'

'Percival? I've heard that name before.'

'Who hasn't? Evil son-of-a-four-leg,' says Bonzo under his breath.

'What's Percival got to do with Bluebell?' asks Noah.

'Well, for starters,' says Lord Hamish, 'he's sitting right next to her on Live TV.'

Noah gulps so hard, he almost chokes on his saliva.

61

'Are you telling me that the much-feared Mr Percival is a blooming standard poodle?'

'You got it in one,' says Phil.

— CHAPTER SIX —

A Lupine Apparition

Too many questions, too few answers: Noah wishes his brain came with a pause button. Will Bluebell recognise him if they meet again? Might she prefer to stay put in her new home than come with him? Is Percival Poodle as bad as everybody says he is, considering how well Bluebell looks? How is Percival Poodle getting away with keeping company with a genuine dog of doggy habits? Is he above the law? Is he the law?

Noah knows if he can't find a way to escape from Roomdaorb, he's wasting brain space on these questions. So what would it take for a 'mutant' like him to travel unseen to the capital city of Nod Nol where Percival Poodle lives? Whom could he trust? What would he eat? Where would he sleep? What if a virus infected him, one against which his body had no immunity? Are there poisonous spiders, snakes, scorpions, or disease-bearing mosquitoes? Are there grizzly bears, tigers, hippopotamuses, elephants, or crocodiles?'

On the way to the canteen for tea, he decides to pump Nursing Assistant Charlie for information, taking advantage of his good mood over Lambast City thrashing Yarridge West, six goals to one. Noah starts with some general chat about the football match. He then steers the conversation towards the subject of half-time and the 'distinguished-looking' Percival Poodle.

'Mr Poodle is top of the Rich List,' says Charlie. 'He owns every building in Nod Nol City and all of its suburbs. Even Central Government has to pay him rent for their offices and debating halls.'

'But aren't governments meant to own their own buildings?' Noah asks.

'Nobody really knows what happened to bring about this odd change in ownership, but it's rumoured that the Government got into such debt it had to sell its buildings to Mr Poodle, and rent them back off him.'

'How does the Prime Minister feel about this?'

Charlie glances at the nearest security guard, not answering Noah's question until they are out of his earshot. 'The PM minds a great deal, what with Mr Poodle increasing the rent whenever he disapproves of a new bill being passed through Parliament.'

'Unofficially then, Percival is the one in charge?'

'That is what he likes to think, but everyone secretly feels sorry for the PM. It's no fun for her having an ill-bred property tycoon calling all the shots—especially one who'd dearly love to take over her job.'

'What's the Prime Minister called?'

'The Right Honourable Miranda Airedale Terrier.'

They reach the canteen now. Charlie ends the conversation and wanders off to engage in a bit of football banter with a staff nurse, Tom Pointer, who's a supporter of Yarridge West.

Noah goes to stand next to Goldie in the food queue, bracing himself to relieve her of yet another helping of pineapple from her plate. Despite reminding himself of the health benefits of the fruit, this evening's rank offering of grilled liver and pineapple sandwich looks the biggest challenge to his taste buds so far.

He and Goldie go to sit at a table with Jimmy Whippet, Dorothy Dalmatian, and Bonzo Bulldog. There are no security guards in the canteen, and no other nursing staff other than Charlie and Tom, who are too busy chatting to overhear any other conversations.

Noah takes the opportunity to quiz Jimmy about a few things. 'A little bird tells me that you're a whizz at stealing, and very fast on the feet.'

'Pretty much so.'

'How are you at lock-picking?'

'Depends on what sort.'

'The microchipped sort.'

'Even if I knew the answer to that—which I don't— why should I trust a mutant like you with insider info? Phoebe Watson's the same as you, give or take a few details. She's also the worst fly-by-night character anyone could meet.'

'You mean there's a real-live girl in the Zyx-dimension. How come nobody has mentioned her to me before, in all the time I've been here?'

'I ain't calling her a girl. More like an old crone. They've probably not mentioned her as they don't realise you're the same species, seeing as you look so different and you're so much nicer than she is.'

'Where do I find her? I'm thinking of getting out of this place, you see.'

Jimmy throws his paw-hands up in the air. 'Ha, fat chance of that!' He grins at Noah as if he believes him a

65

genuine nutter.

Noah turns to Bonzo. 'You remember you mentioned Horticulture the other day, or, more importantly, the mud there?'

'Yes. What of it?'

'In my world, people have been known to dig their way out of secure prisons and concentration camps.'

Jimmy screws up his pointed snout with a hard-to-convince look. 'And did they have to swim piranha-infested waters, too?'

'What? In this lake? More like a rumour put about by the staff to frighten us.' Noah remembers watching a nature film about these flesh-eating fish—how they like to travel in huge shoals, often near the surface. He's about eighty-percent certain he would have seen them from out of a hospital window by now, although the remaining twenty-percent of doubt could prove fatal.

Goldie polishes off the final morsel of her pineapple-free sandwich and gives her paw-hand a sneaky lick. 'I know exactly how to get into Horticulture, but first Jimmy needs to steal a magnet from somewhere.'

'And how might I do that, Miss Smarty-pants Retriever?' he asks.

'You tell me. You're the expert thief. Or is that a false rumour, too?'

'Cheek of it. I'll unzip you here and now, if you question my thieving skills.'

Noah has no idea what Jimmy means by unzipping Goldie, but, reading from the startled expression on her face, it cannot be nice.

<><><>

Noah decides it's time to do a bit of concentrated piranha spotting from on high. By luck, an opportunity arises for a jaunt up to Dr Borzoi's private rest room on the second floor the following weekend. On this particular Saturday, the staffing level is at an all-time low with only five security guards and three members of the nursing staff on duty.

Jimmy says everyone has signed off sick to attend the Cup Final live between Lambast City and Looprevil United. Of those who've bothered to turn up for work, seven have just retired to the day room half-an-hour before kick-off, armed with fizzy drinks and packets of dried-fish crispies. This leaves only an agency nurse named Fliss Beagle, who, according to Tamara Beagle, is as dim as an overcooked potato and no relative of hers.

'Fliss won't get in the way of what we want to do,' Jimmy assures Noah. 'I've just seen her disappear off into a quiet room, armed with glossy mags, a huge box of candied bananas, and her manicure set.'

Jimmy takes Noah to an unlocked utility room. On a hook, hidden behind a bucket under the sink, are a couple of ornate iron keys more suited to a castle door than to a hi-tech modern secure unit. It seems Dr Borzoi has a fascination for antiquities, as well as for old-fashioned habits, such as leaving his keys in a stupid place for the convenience of visiting burglars.

Outside a door marked STRICTLY PRIVATE, Jimmy hands Noah the keys. 'I'll keep yow.'

'Yow?'

'Yeah, I'll keep watch down here, while you nose around upstairs. If Fliss Beagle appears, I'll knock her off your scent with a bit of the old smooth chat.'

'Okay. I get you.'

The first key grates a bit in the lock and then turns with rather too loud a clunk for Noah's comfort. The whole set-up seems about as rigged as a reality TV show. Gloom shadows the stairwell to Borzoi's rest room. A standard old-fashioned light bulb hangs from the ceiling at the foot of the stairs and another one at the top. They are both dead when Noah tests them from the rocker switch on the wall. He imagines the doctor creeping up the stairs to his retreat armed with an old-fashioned torch, complete with disposable batteries.

Leaving the door ajar a small amount, Noah starts to climb up the stairs and walks smack into a spider's web, which engulfs his face and sticks a plump purple spider on the end of his nose. He squeezes his lips tight, snatches at the spider, and plucks it off him. As the creatures scuttles away at a lopsided angle, Noah pales and shudders at the thought of how different the outcome for him if the spider had been poisonous; he would have been in the throes of agony or dead by now.

He continues up the stairs with caution, brushing away any webs in his path with the keys. At the door to Dr Borzoi's rest room, he tries the second key in the lock, but it refuses to budge after half a turn. He notices the door handle fixture is upside down and needs lifting rather than pushing down. *Perhaps, this means the lock works back to front as well.* He tries the key again, turning it clockwise this time and finds success.

The room beyond is huge, with panoramic windows all down one side. On the three remaining sides are wall paintings of a Mediterranean-looking holiday resort, full of adult dog-people and their pup-children chilling out on sandy beaches, doing exactly the things humans do on beaches: sunbathing, going for a dip in the sea, eating ice creams, playing with buckets and spades, throwing beach balls etc.

The room contains little by way of furniture: just a

striped folding deckchair and a low table on which sits a transistor radio, an empty ice bucket, and a paperback book. But more interestingly, there's a telescope on a stand in front of the window.

Noah crosses the sand-coloured tile floor to take a closer look.

The height of the telescope might suit the tall Dr Borzoi, but Noah has to balance his feet on a metal cuff around the stand—about 50 centimetres from its base— to raise him up to the correct viewing height. To his irritation, its blurred lens takes an age to focus but it seems Jimmy was right about the doctor banning security cameras from his retreat.

Training the telescope on the lake, Noah sees heaped white clouds reflected upon its calm surface, their deep descent into the water looking like another world in reverse. What if the lake contains a portal, which leads to yet another unexplored dimension? There are no piranhas travelling the watery cloud landscape, although he supposes they could be anywhere at any given moment in a lake of this size.

He shifts his line of sight to the distance, north-west from where he stands and in the direction of the capital, Nod Nol City. It's impossible to make out much other than the tops of possible skyscrapers, masts, and electricity pylons, which look as unreachable as a desert mirage. By the time he finds Bluebell, she'll have aged into an old dog with stiff joints and a grey snout.

This is the second time in his life the Fates have robbed him of something he really loves: first his mum, and now his puppy. He can't decide who is worse out of the ridiculous Percival Poodle, or that child-hating Kate that Dad inflicted upon him less than six months after Mum died. He hopes, if he perishes in the process of

69

stealing Bluebell back from Percival, his ghost can jump dimensions and haunt Kate as a poltergeist whose specialty is trashing shopping.

His anger blots out the sun, stirs up the lake, and sets the whole room vibrating, or that's how it seems as a fuzzy greyness replaces his view of the rooftops and masts of distant Nod Nol City. He looks away from the eyepiece of the telescope and tumbles off his perch in shock. Staring through the window at him is a grey lupine face belonging to a creature of at least nine metres tall.

The giant dog-man grins at him, displaying a set of teeth with canines like kitchen knives. Taking a piece of paper as big as a bath towel out of his pocket, he scribbles a message on it, and holds it up to the window for Noah to read.

> *You find a way out of the hospital after dark on a moonless night, and I'll see you across the water in no time. Signed, Finn McDrool Irish Wolfhound.*

— CHAPTER SEVEN —

Miss Fluffball Pomeranian's Worst Nightmare

Jimmy says, 'Guess who Noah thinks he's just seen?'
Noah gives Jimmy a shove, annoyed at his teasing. 'You're jealous, that's all. It's not everyday someone has a legendary giant seek him out.'

'Okay, calm down. I know you're desperate to get out of here, but—'

'Oooooooooo, too scary,' interrupts Goldie, breaking into a fit of the quivers. 'Those giants roar and stamp you underfoot. Nightmare *m-m*-monsters … fantasy creations. Most, most, most absolutely pretend.'

Noah clutches at his head in exasperation. 'Not you, too. Do you want to leave this place, or not? Don't chicken out now. You agreed to come. Trust me, it was definitely Finn McDrool I saw, and he wasn't scary.'

'I believe you, mate,' says Phil Labrador.

'Thanks, Phil. I appreciate it.' They exchange a high-five.

Goldie clears her throat and manages a nervous smile. 'I found a *m-m*-magnet on Doctor Borzoi's desk.'

'How can you possibly have done that?' asks

71

Tamara Beagle, curling her lip scornfully.

'He called me to his office to check how *my-my*-my levels of stress are responding to therapy.'

Lord Hamish lets out a disgusted snort. 'I think we'd all suffer less stress if the Doctor took early retirement.'

'Where's the magnet, now?' asks Bonzo.

'It's still on his desk, I expect.'

'What, in Zyx's name, is the use of that?'

'Borzoi had his eyes on me the whole time I was there, otherwise I *m-m*-might've put it in my pocket.'

A plan formulates in Noah's head. It involves a diversion and Jimmy doing a spot of thievery. 'Leave it to me,' he says, as if it's the easiest thing in the world to outwit a dog-psychiatrist who's less sane than his patients are.

<><><>

Noah confirms through gossip that, indeed, Dr Borzoi has an addiction to ancient artefacts, antiques, and collectables, ninety-nine percent of which he'll never use.

The psychiatrist refuses modern technology in his office: no desktop or laptop computer; no fax machine, scanner or photocopier; no security cameras. He does have a 1920s-style black telephone with a dial but it isn't connected to a line.

His poor secretary, Miss Fluffball Pomeranian, armed with a pen and shorthand pad, has to take down his erratic dictations, and then type his letters on an old manual typewriter in the adjoining room. Through the wall, visitors to the psychiatrist's office often hear the sound of the typewriter's clickety-clack keys and the bell-ping of its carriage return, as well as an occasional frustrated sob from Miss Fluffball, followed by an energetic screwing up of paper.

Dr Borzoi shouts at the poor secretary daily about her terrible spelling, but she dare not suggest to him that he buy her a word processor with a spelling and grammar checker. The plus side of this is that Dr Borzoi has no computer hard drives to de-magnetise; otherwise he wouldn't dare have a magnet anywhere near his desk.

<><><>

Two days after the discussion about the magnet, Jimmy Whippet engineers a one-to-one conversation with Dr Borzoi, which he proudly recounts to Noah later.

His story goes something like this (*give or take a bit of exaggeration*)...

The psychiatrist sits opposite Jimmy, both elbows on his desk, his right eye peering out of a monocle.

Jimmy pretends to submit to the psychiatrist, letting him win the staring contest. This kills two birds with one stone by allowing Dr Borzoi to believe he's the one in control, while Jimmy can scan the desk for the magnet without raising suspicion.

At first, all Jimmy can see spread before him is a sea of chaos consisting of disorganised papers, academic journals, golfing magazines, and heavy textbooks, two of which are open and taking up a sizeable area of the desk.

After a long silence, the psychiatrist asks him 'What is your trouble, Master Whippet?'

'Compulsion,' replies Jimmy. 'I've this irresistible urge to nick stuff all the time, although, more often than not, I return it after.'

'Well, that is a small amount of progress.'

'But how do I finish with the urge, before anything grabs me fancy?'

'I could arrange for you to attend some sessions of

73

assertiveness therapy.'

'Never heard of it.'

'In simple terms, it is about learning to say "no" to temptation.'

'Sounds way too religious for me.'

'I am not in the business of religion, Master Whippet. Psychiatry pays better. I like my creature comforts, so to speak.'

'All right for some.'

'Young fellow, it is not "all right for some" when there are burglars around to steal our creature comforts off us.'

'So when do I start my therapy?'

Following Jimmy's failure to spot the magnet during his one-to-one with Dr Borzoi, Noah decides to create a diversion during the first therapy session.

It is common knowledge around the hospital that Miss Fluffball Pomeranian is terrified of large spiders. By some glad coincidence, for the last few days arachnids fitting that description have been climbing up through the plughole of the bath Noah usually uses.

Today's count reveals twelve juicy fat house spiders, with leg spans of between three and five centimetres apiece, now trapped by Noah in plastic containers nicked from out of the canteen bins.

Rumours fly about Roomdaorb as fast as electricity through cables. One such rumour is that a poisonous spider called a Black Tango once bit Fluffball on the end of her nose and she had to take a year-and-a-half off work to mend her frayed nerves; although she still isn't completely better, judging by her habit of screwing paper up into balls and sobbing.

The only way to gain access to the secretary is via

Dr Borzoi's office, set up this way on purpose as he's a control freak. But Noah's plan doesn't require full access to the secretary's office: just to the wall-hatch in the corridor outside the room that's used for postal delivery and collection, as well as for passing sandwiches and cakes to her at regular intervals.

Noah checks the corridor. No security guards, and three minutes spare as far as the cameras are concerned. He transfers twelve spiders from individual pots into a tubular cardboard container, then dashes to the wall-hatch and shoves the open end of the tube through, giving its other end a succession of hard slaps.

With only a second or two to spare, he removes the tube and sprints away, only slowing down as the first of Miss Fluffball's yapping screams reach him. He carries on up the corridor at a lazy pace, as if it's nothing to do with him, while two security guards thunder past him in the direction of Dr Borzoi's office.

His mission complete, Noah can't help feeling sorry for Miss Fluffball Pomeranian for becoming a victim of necessity. An hour later (ZDT), Jimmy fills him in on what happened next, although Noah suspects it's an even more exaggerated account than the one following Jimmy's pre-therapy conversation with Dr Borzoi.

<><><>

At the first yap-scream from Fluffball, Dr Borzoi picks up one of his large books and slams it down on the desk. 'What the blazes is the matter with that silly fluff-brain of a secretary, now?'

'Hormones,' says Jimmy.

'I didn't ask you!'

'Yes, you did.'

'You really must learn the difference between real questions and rhetorical ones.'

Jimmy is about to give Dr Borzoi further lip, when he remembers his reason for being there. 'Perhaps you should go and check her out.'

'Do not go telling me my job.'

'Okay.'

Two security guards try to charge through the office door at once, with their guns drawn, and Jimmy thinks how funny it would be if they shot each other while attempting to be first on the scene.

'Would you please be good enough to knock next time,' the psychiatrist says to them.

They both show Jimmy the muzzles of their guns. One of them bellows at him, 'What you playing at whippersnapper?' And the other threatens him with solitary confinement.

Jimmy holds up both of his paw-hands. 'Not guilty!'

'Through here,' Dr Borzoi says to the guards. Before disappearing out of view into his secretary's office, he turns and points a warning claw-finger at Jimmy. 'You stay put. Don't move a muscle and don't touch anything.'

Jimmy salutes him. 'No sir, certainly not sir.'

A second or two later, Borzoi begins yelling. 'How in Zyx's name did these get in here? Remove them. Stamp on them. Shoot them if necessary, but just get them out of here.'

A great deal of banging, crashing, and swearing follows, which Jimmy imagines is caused by the security guards chasing the spiders around the floor, up the walls, and standing on bits of furniture to putt at them on the ceiling. All the while, Fluffball alternates between shrieking, sobbing, and whimpering.

In an attempt to calm her, Dr Borzoi tries the tough

approach first and tells her to pull herself together immediately. When this doesn't work, the psychiatrist slaps her around the face and she becomes even more hysterical. Finally, he tries the gentle approach. 'There, there, there, Miss Pomeranian, it's alright now. They are only common house spiders.'

Hearing this, the secretary wails like a siren.

Jimmy is tempted to abandon his task and see if he can have more success in consoling her, but reminds himself of the importance of his mission. He starts to search for the magnet, peering under books, rifling through a single letter rack, and pressing his paw-hands down on top of the papers strewn across the desk. When he comes across something solid and lumpy, he checks it out, being careful to leave the papers as he finds them afterwards. He discovers a broken eraser, a pencil sharpener, a stapler, a paperweight, and a letter opener, but no magnet.

Next door, things are calming down far too fast for his liking. *Where, where, where was the blessed thing?* He wants to kick himself for not having asked Goldie what size the magnet is. To his relief, Fluffball falls into a further fit of yapping and screaming, buying him more time.

'Just take some deep breaths,' Dr Borzoi tells her. 'Visualise your office returned to a spider-free zone.'

'But one might be lurking inside … *sob* … my typewriter … *sob* … or hiding in my waste … *gulp* … paper basket, or maybe slipped through one of … *cough* … the keyholes in my … *whimper* … desk.'

'Miss Pomeranian, do not worry. I will personally see to it that there are no spiders hiding in your office.'

'What about the hatch? What if more come through?'

'A carpenter can nail it up.'

'What about my sandwiches, and the post?'

Dr Borzoi loses his patience again. 'For crying out-loud, you silly female, use my office for deliveries and collections ... anything. What a carry on about a few house spiders. Just shut up, I say. Just shut up!'

Jimmy is about to abandon his search, when his eyes alight upon an iron door-wedge. He rushes to grab the wedge, expecting the psychiatrist to storm out of his secretary's office any moment. Sweeping it over the papers on the desk, a couple of sheets leap up and stick to its base, clamped there by the horseshoe-shaped magnet beneath their reverse sides.

CHAPTER EIGHT

The Chairman Gets Microchipped

An escape committee consisting of Miss Suzie 'Goldie' Golden Retriever, Lord Hamish MacScottish Terrier, Jimmy Whippet, and Bonzo Bulldog, elect Noah as chairman.

Hamish suggests the whole group—including non-committee members—should swear an oath of secrecy. They seal this oath by jabbing themselves with a paperclip and adding a drop of blood to a shared sheet of white paper. Noah asks to go first, not out of bravery, but because he's scared of picking up an alien disease from sharing a paperclip with the others.

The first committee meeting takes place an hour after tea in the gymnasium. A security guard watches them through reinforced glass from the gallery above, so they start by running about, pretending to play basketball while passing ideas between them. After a respectable length of time, they take a breather, lounging about on a pile of rubber mats in the corner, sipping water out of white polystyrene cups.

'The best time to make a run for it is when the

ZFSC final's on telly,' says Jimmy. 'It'll be dark at twenty-five o'clock—a couple of hours before the programme starts—with moonrise not due until twenty past thirty-six.'

'What and when is the ZFSC?' asks Noah. 'I suppose it's another stupid football match, with that stupid, stupid, stupid poodle posing for the telly cameras.'

Jimmy lets out a loud laugh. 'Nah, it's even more stupid than that. It's the Zyx Federation Song Contest. And it takes place on Saturday week.'

The security guard knocks at the window with his truncheon and wags a disapproving paw-finger at them all.

'Killjoy,' Jimmy mutters under his breath. 'We'd better get back to our game.'

They toss the ball around a bit, until the security guard loses interest in them and goes for a wander up and down, whistling to himself tunelessly.

'So everyone is glued to this song contest, totally?' asks Noah.

'Yes, everyone,' says Bonzo.

The others all nod in agreement.

'Okay,' Noah says, 'so we've agreed on a time. What are we going to do about provisions, clothing, and disguises?'

'A master thief in your midst,' says Jimmy, 'leave it to me.'

Goldie sidles up to Noah. 'Stick your hand in my side-pocket. I want to show you something.'

He thinks it an odd request, but does as asked. It's empty with a hole in the bottom.

'Dig deeper,' says Goldie.

Beyond the tear in her pocket, he comes across a

bumpy metallic strip. 'Is that what I think it is—a zip fastener?'

'It is.'

<><><>

Goldie takes Noah to the 'prosthetics' wardrobe, where her chic little friend, Sally Chihuahua works. While the two dog-girls have a chinwag, Noah wanders about and assesses the stock.

He has learnt that Goldie suffers from stress-induced baldness and has to wear a fun fur Golden Retriever suit until her coat grows back. As this is quite a common disorder amongst Roomdaorb patients, there's a large stock of fur suits to call upon in an emergency. Some of the suits are old ones left behind by cured patients allowed to leave the hospital; other suits are brand new.

Having walked up and down the rows of suits, Noah alights upon a Chow fun fur. It's reddish-gold and of a dense, soft, and springy texture. He removes the suit from its rail and goes to stand in front of a full-length mirror, holding it up against himself. When he realises Sally is looking at him, he strokes the suit and says in a twittish voice, 'It's *so, so, so* lov-e-ly and soft.'

'Don't mind him,' Goldie says to Sally. 'He's undergoing treatment at the moment and Dr Borzoi has temporarily addled his brains.'

<><><>

Out in the corridor once more, Noah and Goldie run into Jimmy, who's sloping along, looking very glum, with the corners of his mouth downturned and his shoulders hunched.

'What's wrong with you?' Noah asks.

'Not now. Later. The walls have ears.'

At recreation time, Noah retires to the table tennis

81

room to play doubles with Jimmy, Bonzo, and Goldie. The room has no windows for security guards to look through, but it has cameras. The four friends decide to limit their conversation either to when they swap ends, or to when the balls need collecting up.

As they bend down to retrieve the first batch of balls, Jimmy says to Noah, 'It don't work.'

'What doesn't?'

'The magnet. It don't trash the electronics like we thought. And the blimming door won't budge.'

Bonzo sticks his head under the table, exposing the pink linings of his crumpled velvet jowls. 'How dare you test it without telling us first? Are we a committee, or are we not?'

'I'd keep your voice down, if I were you,' says Goldie.

Bonzo scowls at her. 'Well, you're not me.'

After they've resumed their game of table tennis, a new idea comes to Noah. At the next opportunity, he asks Jimmy, 'Where did the patients who work here, such as Sybil Spaniel, get their paws microchipped?'

'In the clinic room next to Utility, where we got the keys.'

'Do they store spare microchips in there?'

Jimmy doesn't know the answer to this question. He checks with Goldie, but she's none the wiser.

'What about you, Bonzo?' Noah asks.

He scratches the top of his head with the handle of the ping-pong bat. 'Well, from what I've heard, a standard issue microchip has a universal rather than a personalised number and only gives access to low security areas.'

'Interesting, but it doesn't answer my question?'

'Yes, it does. It means there's a good chance there

are boxes of them stashed down in the main stores along with everyday hospital supplies.'

'That's where Dorothy Dalmatian works,' says Goldie. 'I'm sure we can include her in our escape plans and trust her to keep quiet. All we need to do is bribe her with the promise of chasing, roughing, and tumbling in the fields with Phil Labrador when we get out of here.'

Noah keeps watch outside, while Goldie and Tamara distract Sally Chihuahua with a bit of girl-chat as Jimmy sneaks into the prosthetics wardrobe.

Ten minutes later—with the help of a few cushions, some fleecy off-cuts, and his rolled up boiler suit— Jimmy reappears as a decently plumped up Chow-fellow in an up-sized boiler suit. He ignores Noah and carries on along the corridor, adopting a depressed plod for the benefit of two security guards coming in the other direction.

Noah nurses his smarting hand. 'Ouch, ouch, ouch! You deserve to get bitten for that, MacScottish. You told me you'd done microchipping before, when it's obvious you haven't.'

Lord Hamish peers at Noah from beneath heavy brows. 'Sorry, young fellow. You're my first live candidate. In the past, I practised on a citrus flame fruit during my time of doing Compulsory Federation Service in the Army Medical Corps.'

I will never, never, never let anyone do that to me again, even if I return to my own dimension and it is made law for every British citizen to be microchipped— especially bearing in mind they'd treat me as an alien spy if they discovered a Zyx-microchip in my left-hand.

CHAPTER NINE

Horticulture

Saturday night: Noah watches the bedside clock square its way to twenty-seven hours ZDT. Eight minutes to go; Lord Hamish beats out the elongated seconds on the iron-frame of his bed with his toothbrush. They have chosen this room for their rendezvous for the following reasons:

1. **There's only one short flight of stairs downwards between it and Horticulture.**

2. **It's a spacious private room, as Hamish is very rich.**

3. **Private rooms have no surveillance cameras, unless you count the one in the en-suite teliot—doubtless put there for Dr Borzoi's entertainment.**

4. **Private patients have the privilege of keeping snacks and cans of drink in their bedside cupboard.**

5. **There are duvets on the beds in place of standard-issue starched sheets and prickly blankets. A duvet is a good hiding-place for an all-in-one Chow fun fur and a spare one-piece suit.**

6. The main day room with the best telly is at the far end of the building from Lord Hamish's room.

The stress of waiting starts to affect certain members of the escape party in ways Noah finds worrying.

Goldie is panting profusely, which is a dog's alternative to sweating, and her eyes are bulging in fright. Dorothy Dalmatian cannot stop talking, but stops when Bonzo shouts at her to shut up. Phil Labrador is jumping on and off Hamish's bed, bark-singing a Zyx equivalent of R'n'B while doing some impressive moves.

Tamara says to Noah, 'Wait until Phil gets out his tail and really boogies-on-down. Showing the tail is considered a teenage rebellion thing, which doesn't become illegal until adulthood.'

Hamish glances at his watch. 'One minute to go, and counting. Noah, you'd better call the troops to attention.'

Noah claps his hands and hisses at everyone to shush. To his surprise, they obey him. Now it's almost too quiet but for the distant sound of the telly.

'Not happy,' says Minnie Jack Russell in a high-pitched squeak.

'Why? You got cold feet, or something?' asks Phil.

She twitches her nose, so her whiskers vibrate like wire antennae. 'Not happy because something don't smell right around here.'

'*Doesn't* smell right,' says Hamish.

'Don't you "doesn't" me, MacScottish. It don't smell right, so there.'

'Do shush, both of you,' says Noah. 'It isn't the time for arguing. What exactly is the problem, Minnie?'

Tamara sniggers. 'Phil's armpits, most likely.'

85

Minnie points at the door, mouthing, 'We've got company.'

A minute later, a beefy security guard barges in on them. 'Nice cosy little party,' he says with a sneer, folding his lips back over his teeth and displaying his gums. His left canine tooth flashes gold, posing as a precious metal implant but more likely cheap bling.

Noah feels his cheeks reddening, but Bling-tooth ignores him, more interested in Goldie's noisy panting and the saliva streaming out of her mouth.

'What's eating you, miss?' he asks.

Goldie's eyes dart around the room. A gurgling noise comes out of her throat but no words.

'That false coat of hers has too high a density rating,' says Tamara. 'She's waiting for a lighter one from Prosthetics.'

The security guard marches over to within an arm's length of Tamara, clicks the heels of his knee-high boots together, and towers over her in a threatening manner. 'Okay, Miss Beagle, since you've elected yourself spokesperson, perhaps you'd like to tell me why you lot ain't watching the ZFSC on the box, like the rest of us?'

Noah blurts out, 'But *you're* not watching it, sir.'

Bling-tooth sucks in his cheeks, swivels around on his heels, and wags a paw-finger at him. 'Respect your elders!'

'Sorry sir.' Noah resists pointing out that, timewise, he has probably been alive longer than Bling-tooth has.

The security guard manages a grin, its effect far more alarming than his sneering and cheek sucking. 'That's more like it. As for why I'm not watching the box—I ain't having me eardrums assaulted by a load of wet songs. It's iron-heads music or nuffink for me, ta very much.'

86

Heavy-metal music, Noah guesses. 'Yeah, I don't like all that wet and girlie stuff either,' he says, hoping to curry favour. But it works too well, and Bling-tooth slumps down on the side of Lord Hamish's bed, looking set to stick with them the whole evening.

'Ain't you going to pour me a drink, then?' He scans their faces, ending up with fixing upon Goldie. 'You look, for one, like you could kill a drink, Missy.'

Lord Hamish disappears into the bathroom and returns with a toothbrush mug full of cold water.

Bling-tooth eyes the offering with disgust. 'Give me somethink from your stash right now, you toffee-nosed what's-it, or I'll turn the place over and put an end to your little party.'

Noah's heart skips some beats, as Lord Hamish spirits a can of fizzy drink out of his bedside cupboard and tosses it over too fast for the security guard to get a proper look at their travel supplies.

Bling-tooth tugs the aluminium ring-pull open with his mouth and a load of foam erupts out of the top of the can, down his chin. He takes a long swig of drink, lets out a loud belch, and wipes his mouth with the back of his paw-hand. 'I'm feeling disposed towards a spot of entertainment now? Master Padgett, sing us somethink with a dose of iron to it.'

A karaoke evening is not what Noah has in mind. He hates singing—except on his own, plugged into headphones—but he senses he must play the game, or else...

He does some *d-d-d-der-ring* of a baddie tune from one of his computer games, which appears to meet with approval. Bling-tooth slurps down the remainder of his drink, belches again, and stands up. Clicking his heels together, he shakes Noah by the hand. 'Good stuff that,

87

but work to do. See you later.'

As the door closes behind the security guard, Noah tries to interpret what 'later' means. Back home it can mean anything from an hour to a whole year, depending upon who says it.

<><><>

Jimmy pokes his nose out the door first. He sniffs the air to the right, to the left, and to the right again. 'All clear,' he reports.

Lord Hamish snatches up his clock. 'We have two minutes to get down those stairs and into Horticulture before the security cameras catch us.'

Bonzo takes hold of a canvas bag stuffed to bursting with high-energy cereal bars, carrot chews, and dried banana; all nicked by Jimmy from the hospital stores, along with the rest of their supplies. Phil hoists over his shoulder a canvas bag containing canned drinks and nine water bottles. Noah slings on a backpack, which strains at the buckles and seams to contain his bulky Chow suit. He has also squeezed in a bag of Inky Everlasting Gobstoppers, otherwise known as IEG sweets, to stain his tongue the correct colour for a Chow.

The corridor looks a hundred times longer than usual, with the top of the stairs a distant fortress. At the sight of it, Noah's legs seem to weigh fifty kilograms each. He snatches at dense air, his stomach coiled into a knot. There's a smell of hot emulsion paint, linoleum flooring, and disinfectant. It reminds him of school and the stifling corridor leading to the main hall for end-of-term exams.

Allowing the others to go first, he forces himself after them. Only as they disappear out of sight down the stairs, does he realise Goldie isn't with them. With less than a minute spare, he looks back and sees Goldie pinned to the wall in panic. Despite his desperation to escape, he returns and grabs her by the paw-hand.

She wriggles, taking a nip at him.

'You want to stay here forever, or what?' he hisses at her.

She whimpers and looks down at the floor. 'Yes, I think I do.'

'Well, I don't, so stop being so selfish and pull yourself together.'

Her paw-hand relaxes in his grip. 'If you say so, Noah.'

The camera whirs; it's seconds away from immortalising his and Goldie's failed escape on film. They dash headlong, and tumble over each other all the way down the stairs to the bottom. Noah's backpack breaks his fall. Phil catches hold of Goldie, tearing either her clothing or the fur suit underneath.

Lord Hamish looks at his clock. 'Hate to say it, young fellow, but I think you were two seconds too late. You should have left her there.'

'No way.'

'Come on, zip it up,' says Jimmy with a snarl, his pointed noise as sharp as a swordfish. 'We've got work to do. Get yourself over here, Noah, and give us a hand.'

Noah places the cushioned part of his palm on the scanner for it to read his microchip. Something beeps, and the door to Horticulture opens with a click. They all dash inside not a moment too soon, as the door is on a timer and closes automatically behind them, almost trapping Noah's backpack in it.

Once inside, they come up against two unforeseen problems straight away. The sprinklers are on and there's zero light.

'You'd need to eat five kilos of carrots a day to see past the end of your nose in here,' says Noah. This makes him think of Bluebell. Perhaps if Percival Poodle makes a habit of giving her a bag of carrots a day, she'll end up wanting to stay with him rather than return home? He brushes the idea aside before it gets a full hold over him.

Bonzo produces a small torch hidden amongst his food supplies, flicks it on, and shoves it at Noah. 'Hold this while I dig.'

As the bulldog-man gets down on all fours and sets to work shifting earth, Goldie lets out an alarmed cry, nearly making Noah drop the torch.

Jimmy goes up close to her face and clacks his teeth at her. 'Shut it, or else.'

Phil shoulders him aside. 'Hey, mate, don't talk to her like that.' He asks Goldie in a gentle voice, 'What's eating you, honeybun?'

'No, no eating. There's p-p-pine—'

'Pineapples, are you trying to say?'

'Oh don't, please don't speak the word.' She wails loud as a siren and swoons into Phil's arms.

Noah strains to listen beyond the falling of artificial rain and the beating of his heart. He expects to hear boots marching on linoleum towards their door, but there's nothing.

Minnie Jack Russell asks Goldie, 'Peaches—you were trying to say peaches, weren't you?'

'Or pomegranates,' says Tamara.

'How about pears?' Phil asks.

'Well, I think I saw some parsnip-tops over by the far wall,' says Noah while training the torch on Bonzo for him to resume digging.

Lord Hamish snorts. 'Since when did you have

better nocturnal vision than us lot?'

'My vitamin A reserves have kicked in suddenly.'

Dorothy Dalmatian starts to leap about and bark with excitement. 'Peas, plums, primroses, and plankton, periwinkles, porcupines, pepper, plaice, pretzels, pasta, parmesan, parcel tape—'

Jimmy cuts her off. 'I'll parcel tape your snout if you don't button it up first. Now everyone shut it up and focus.'

By now, all that's left of Bonzo above ground level are his muscled flanks, rear-end, and tail-stump. He continues to work flat-out, without once emerging for air. Watching his tremendous progress, Noah begins to feel stirrings of hope, but the hope is short-lived.

Bonzo erupts backwards out of his tunnel, shouting, 'Mulch, mulch, mulch,' or rather, 'Ouch, ouch, ouch,' with his mouth full of mud and muck. Blood drips from his jowls. He pushes aside the torch, to stop Noah shining it in his face. 'Go easy on a fellow when he's just broken several teeth for nothing.' He spits out a mouthful of bloody mud, grit, compost, and tooth fragments.

Minnie asks, 'Shall I carry on where you've left off digging?'

'Not unless you want to end up toothless, too. It's solid concrete down there.'

Noah can't believe how dense they've all been, or maybe it was just a case of extreme wishful thinking that this one area of the secure unit would have a bare earth floor and no foundations. Of course that's nonsense; he sees that now. Without concrete foundations throughout, there'd be nothing to hold up the hefty breezeblock walls and stop the building slipping off the island into the lake.

91

Goldie slumps down, clutching at her head, too choked up to manage even a whimper. The rest of them stand gaping at the hole that leads nowhere. To make matters worse, the torch starts to die. At the same time, the terrifying noise arises of marching boots coming in their direction: around half-a-dozen pairs with clickety-clicking steel toecaps, stomping heels, and squeaking leather.

No chance of ever seeing Bluebell again now, thinks Noah. More like solitary confinement, followed by a life sentence for him and his co-conspirators. Terror shreds his insides, as if a swarm of flesh-eating wire butterflies has taken up residence in him.

Goldie cowers, shivering from head to toe. Apart from the torn one-piece suit (that's no longer one-piece) and fun fur, Noah can't see much difference between her and an abused dog in an RSPCA poster. He sits down and strokes her back, in a vain attempt to soothe some of her fears away.

The boots march on relentless: louder and louder, faster and faster.

Bonzo nurses his face between two paw-hands. Jimmy lets out a low growl. Phil scratches at his head in apparent puzzlement. Minnie hunkers down in the concrete-bottomed hole. Dorothy runs up and down, searching for something or anything. Lord Hamish juts out his chin, square beard forward. Only Tamara appears undaunted as she stands with her hands on her hips, looking up at the reinforced glass window.

Noah recalls something from back home about a beagle nicknamed 'Spiderman', capable of scaling a six-metre wall to escape its back yard. This leads him to wonder how many metres from the ground the windows are in Horticulture. About the same, he reckons.

Phil draws a couple of drink cans from out of his backpack. 'We could throw these at the security guards.'

'Fine lot of good those would do against tear-gas and stun guns,' says Jimmy.

'Bebber-ban-boing-bibe-bams-boo-b-baubber,' burbles Bonzo through his fast-swelling lips.

'What's that you just said, Bonzo?' Noah asks.

An invisible Minnie calls out from the bunker, 'Better than going like lambs to the slaughter—that's what he said.'

Tamara drops to the ground, her ears cocked. 'Be quiet everyone. Do you hear it? Can you feel those vibrations?'

'In case you hadn't noticed,' says Phil, 'there's an army of crazed security guards about to hit the place.'

Minnie's head and shoulders emerge from her bunker. 'No, shush! I felt it, too. It's an earthquake.'

Tremors pass through Noah's feet, twanging at his calves, followed by a steady thudding noise that is cross between a hammer drill and the approaching feet of a Tyrannosaurus rex. Instinctively, he curls into a ball and covers the back of his head with his hands.

<><><>

Glass shatters from high up and spikes Noah's back like hailstones. Something huge and hairy scoops him and Goldie off the ground in its paw-hands, while Minnie clings to one of its claws and comes along for the ride.

'Hop-you upon me shoulder, there, and don't y' go wasting me time,' says their rescuer, who Noah recognises as Finn 'McDrool' Irish Wolfhound.

'Oooo, is he safe?' asks Goldie.

Minnie swings herself up onto the leathery palm of his paw-hand, which is as big as the podium of a bandstand. She whispers to Noah, 'Are you sure he's to be trusted? Did you catch a glance of his teeth?'

'Take your pick,' says Noah, aware his voice has risen several tones. 'Either we go with Finn and take the small risk of getting swallowed whole, or stay behind and get torn to shreds by a pack of deranged security guards.'

The giant booms, 'Oh Jemony, Memmani, and Jossopy, get your sorry undersides up here.' He deposits the three of them on the grubby red-tartan shoulder of his coarse cotton shirt.

Noah wrinkles his nose. Finn stinks of stagnant water mixed with manure. The grey hairs of his snout and neck have a yellowish tinge to them, demonstrating a hatred of soap.

'Now, lie yourselves down on me shoulder,' Finn says, 'lest you topple off while I'm rescuing the others.'

Noah does what he's told, drawing a trembling Goldie down with him and keeping her close while clutching at Finn's shirt. His stomach lurches as the giant stoops down and rises in two swift movements, to plonk Tamara, Jimmy, and Bonzo on his far shoulder. From below, Dorothy barks her head off.

Phil yells at her. 'Shut it, spotty!' which makes her bark even louder.

'Cans to the ready, Master Labrador,' Lord Hamish orders him.

'Aye, aye, sir,' replies Phil.

Noah punches Finn on the shoulder. 'Get them out, this minute, or I'll bite you.'

'No need to get your nappies in a twist, baldy features,' says Finn.

The giant bends forward too fast for Noah to put his fists away and regain a proper hold of him. Noah lets out a short shriek as he does a half-somersault through

94

the air, with his backpack attached, to land upside down in Finn's gaping shirt pocket. After battling with a half-eaten biscuit and a gluey crumpled handkerchief for a moment or two, he manages to turn himself the right way up.

Minnie calls down to him. 'You okay, Noah? Goldie has managed to stay put.'

He emerges from the pocket with biscuit crumbs stuck to his face by one of Finn's bogeys. On the verge of puking, Noah replies with sarcasm. 'First class hotel this is. Just remind me to bring back a souvenir.'

A crackling electrical noise comes from below, driving Dorothy into a mania of barking. Phil yells something about stun guns to Lord Hamish; a warning that comes too late, measured by the yowls of pain that follow. Noah holds on extra tight this time, as Finn snatches up both Lord Hamish and Phil, and bungs them into the sticky, crummy pocket with him.

'What about Dorothy?' Noah asks.

A breathless Phil replies. 'She won't stand still for long enough for Finn to grab her. She's doing it purposely, to help us get away.'

Noah shouts at the giant, 'Do something, McDrool, or I'll eat your biscuit.'

'Sorry, me little lad, I've got to get you off this island-here before those frumble-glotting faniocs retire their toy guns in favour of something more lethal.'

As Finn strides away from the island at high speed, Noah looks up at Zyx's crazy-looking star constellations to divert himself from the sound of deep water sloshing about the giant's great feet and legs. How he wished Finn had been around when Mum's car had skidded off that icy bridge into a freezing lake two winters back.

— CHAPTER TEN —

The Arbordral of Faces

Dial-oaks make up the entire forest, and Finn McDrool insists these trees are subtropical evergreens rather than deciduous. Their surface roots create treacherous raised waffle-like patterns on the ground and their branches start about nine-tenths of the way up their trunks, at a height of around fifteen metres, with straight twigs crowning each tree, sticking up in the shape of chimney brushes.

At eye-level, the trunks have gnarled bits of bark formed into the shape of dogs' faces, which is why the forest is nicknamed 'The Arbordral of Faces'. When the wind gets up, the faces seem to move with winking eyes, snarling mouths, flicking ears, and twitching noses.

A hint of a breeze has just thrown Goldie into a major fright. She has glued herself to Noah like a Siamese twin, so their legs tangle after a few paces and the pair of them go sprawling. Still more bruises, he thinks.

'In the past,' says Finn, 'many have come into the forest, never to be seen again, their faces stolen by the trees.'

Goldie stays cowered on the ground. 'Ooo, Noah, you must tell that horrid giant to stop frightening us.'

Noah limps to his feet and pulls himself up as tall as he can, to about three-quarters of the way up the giant's legs. 'Stop frightening her, McDrool. Tell her the Dial-oaks don't eat anyone.'

'Of course they don't. Sorry for scaring you, lass. The trees just like to keep a copy of their guests' faces so they recognise them next time they visit.'

Noah tries to reassure her further. 'The trees are our friends. They've helped keep us alive for the last week, haven't they?'

When Finn first told him about the dial-oaks, he found it hard to believe that something so woody and lacking in foliage could yield so much, but every day the trees go through the same cycle. At dawn, the roots sprout fungi that remain edible until it develops toxic spores two hours after orange sunrise. At midday, if you lie on your back you can catch drops of a nutritious plant-juice tasting of strawberry milkshake, which Noah has nicknamed 'Arbordral-smoothies'. And at pink sunset, the dial-oak's trunks moult pieces of bark tasting of chocolate digestive biscuits.

Even water comes on demand via the trees' taproots that grow downwards from their waffle-roots. You just have to remove the natural corks in their tops to gain access to their underground reservoir, but you must remember to replace the corks afterwards, or the trees' bark-faces will glare at you in unspoken threat.

Goldie's fear of the trees is nothing compared to her terror of bumping into the legendary Phoebe Watson. Finn has said this is unlikely in a forest of nine hundred square kilometres, but Noah knows the giant is yarning.

Why else has he decided to go on vacation to Aisalartsua and instructed him not to wear the Chow suit in case the devilish Ms Watson mistakes him for a member of *Canis sapiens* and tears him to shreds?

Finn has been gone two weeks, with a further week left before he returns. Before his departure, he'd said that there was no point returning until Dr Borzoi had called off the search: a search that most likely would be in the paw-hands of a private firm, as the psychiatrist wouldn't want the authorities knowing how useless he is at his job.

Last night, to the southeast, Noah noticed the smoke of a campfire and the peachy glow of its flames against the sky. It was close enough for the smell of roasting pig to reach him every time the wind picked up.

At first light, he and the others decide to move deeper into the forest, away from their pursuers. They walk until midday, by which time Noah's feet and calf-muscles throb and ache from having waffle-root underfoot. Even when he flops down on the ground onto his back for an Arbordral-smoothie, the pain in his poor, abused limbs continues. He envies his companions, who have no such trouble with their paw-feet. They have the leathery pads of a normal dog, although evolution has lengthened each pad from rounds to long ovals.

After lunch, Phil Labrador decides to practise some new complicated dance moves. This involves some fancy footwork around waffle-roots, accompanied by R'n'B vocals. About a dozen king-size white corkscrew ducks gather to watch the entertainment and quack in appreciation every time Phil does one of his spinning leaps in the air.

These land-dwelling ducks are one of only two

species of creature that are native to this forest. Able to uncork the dial-oaks and re-cork them with their beaks, they are as plump as beanbag cushions, yet capable of extending their legs and necks by about thirty centimetres when they need to do so.

White hammock apes swing about amongst the treetops, making a noise that sounds like 'chitter-chitter-woof-grrrr-yap'. They have dog-like snouts and floppy ears similar to basset hounds. Now and again, they skitter down a tree for a drink and the ducks do the uncorking for them.

One of the apes grins at Noah in a seemingly friendly manner, but Noah remembers Finn warning him about their fits of forest rage. He jumps out of the way and edges back from the creature, before it rips at his flesh with its lethal serrated teeth. Its eyes have gone so crossed its pupils meet like pimples at the bridge of its snout. Throughout Noah's unpleasant encounter, Phil carries on dancing without sign of tiring.

The Labrador-youth's show goes on until the shadows lengthen, by which time the trees have had enough of all the jazz and refuse to donate any bark-biscuits to anyone for supper. The group pack up and move off deeper into the forest, away from the setting sun, their stomachs growling with hunger. A row of corkscrew ducks waddle after them in single file, with their legs and necks adjusted to minimum height. The hammock apes let out eerie howls, as a chill breeze filters between the trees, bringing with it creeping tendrils of fog. Noah shivers and hugs himself for warmth, longing to put on his Chow suit.

'You okay?' Jimmy Whippet asks. 'Your skin has gone as bumpy as a plucked chicken.'

'I feel like a plucked chicken. Finn McDrool wants

me to freeze to death in my flimsy T-shirt.'

'Surely Phoebe Watson would've shown her ugly face by now, if she was real?'

Noah's teeth start to chatter. When he holds his fingers up to his face, they are blue. All he can think about is how snug it would feel inside the Chow fun fur; each time a shiver burrows through him, his will weakens further. To make things worse, the fog suddenly turns so thick, he can't even see Bonzo, who was just in front of him a minute before.

'Can I hold paws with you?' comes Goldie's quavering voice from next to him.

'Sure—why not?' he says, trying to sound braver than he feels for her sake. They carry on blind, with Goldie clutching at him, the quiet packed around him like taped bubble-wrap. He calls back over his shoulder, not really expecting an answer. 'Jimmy, do you think we ought to stop walking and set up camp?'

Silence.

'Jimmy?'

Deeper silence.

'Jimmy? Bonzo? Anyone? Can you hear me?'

Goldie grips at his arm, digging her finger-claws into him. Her breath puffs against his face, smelling acidic and fearful. 'Oh, oh, oh Noah, are we all on our own? Are we t-t-totally l-l-lost?

'Shush. Don't be afraid. I'll look after you.'

The silence has folded in on itself. The wind is on hold. The fog hangs dense as congealed candyfloss. The apes have stopped mid-howl. The ducks are one with the white-out.

<><><>

Noah wonders if he has died and gone to a barren underworld of everlasting fog; an icy hell patrolled by

100

giants far less friendly than Finn McDrool.

He has lost track of time and is weak with hunger. The tree-faces have gone all psycho in the white-out; when he gropes for a dial-oak bark biscuit, he nearly loses his hand. He can't even get a drink, as the trees have sealed their corks.

'I'm going to put on my Chow suit,' he says to Goldie.

She shudders. 'Is that a g-g-good idea?'

'It's all very well for Finn, leaving me to perish from cold and starvation whilst he's busy sunbathing on hot beaches, stuffing himself with four-course dinners, and sleeping in a comfortable bed. This is an emergency. If I die, you'll be on your own.'

'Oh, oh, don't say that. What about Phoebe Watson?'

'Forget her. Help me into this suit.'

Still blinded by the white-out, the two of them scrabble with the fun fur until the head end is at the top and the feet are at the bottom. Noah wriggles into the suit through a stomach flap. When he's fully inside, Goldie fastens down some Velcro-like material for him, and does up a left-hand side-zip. She points out the side-pocket on the right for stashing his IEG sweets.

Clothed in fun fur from head to foot, Noah's fingers and toes prickle painfully as they defrost. Drowsiness soon replaces the discomfort. 'We must rest. We're walking in circles,' he says, barely able to force out his words. Flopping down on his back, he pulls Goldie with him, expecting her to resist, but instead she lets out a long sigh, rests her chin on his shoulder, and drops off to sleep in a blink. Soon her gently rhythmic snores soothe him into a heavy, dreamless sleep, too.

<><><>

If someone had launched him by catapult into the heart of the orange sun, Noah couldn't have suffered a ruder awakening. His *transport* jolts to a halt in the treetops, with a brain-rattling judder, leaving his stomach to follow on after the rest of him. He's on his back in a net-trap, the sun burning through the eye-slits of his fur headpiece.

He turns his head to the right, careful to keep his eyes lined up with the slits. Less than a metre away, a hammock ape swings from a branch by its arms and shows him its teeth. Judging by its cross-eyed expression, Noah decides it's one of those toothy moments unrelated to a friendly grin.

In a trap nearby, Goldie has curled herself up into a ball and is whimpering. He wants to tell her it could be worse, at least they are together, but the words won't come. Last night's fog must have contained an odourless chemical gas and sent them into comas. This was the only explanation for their ensnarement in nets. The least he can do for Goldie is to act calm and not admit his fear of heights, even if he's quaking like a jelly inside.

The floppy-eared ape clacks his serrated teeth and wraps his legs around the branch to bare his hairless rear-end at Noah. A tremendous hullabaloo has turned the forest overnight from a silent grave to a chittering, woofing, howling dog-ape house. It reminds him of feeding time at the zoo. This, combined with the smell of wood-smoke, makes him wonder if he and Goldie are dinner.

'Hey, you,' he yells at the bottom-bearing ape, 'my friend and I both taste of skunk. We're poisonous. If you eat us, you'll die.'

The hammock ape grins and belches loudly, while his fellows nearby swing about, playfully boxing at each other, screeching with delight. A blast from a horn brings their party to an abrupt halt. Noah thinks he can hear the hooves of an approaching horse, but as it moves closer—slowing down from a canter, to a trot, to a walk—he changes his mind about what it is, because he has never heard a horse go *clickety-click*.

When the noise stops beneath his net-trap, it raises gooseflesh on his back inside his Chow suit. He holds his breath, convinced a hammock ape will bite through the rope holding him up and send him plummeting into the jaws of a monster.

A voice calls up, 'Set them down.' It's a honeyed, feminine voice and not at all what Noah would expect to command the respect of a load of deranged hammock apes.

One of the creatures emits an evil chuckle. Noah finds himself dropping headfirst, with the waffle-roots appearing to rush upwards to shatter his skull on impact. About ten centimetres from the ground, the net-trap slams on its brakes.

'Cut them loose,' says his host.

From Noah's landing place, the first thing he sees is four white legs belonging to a tall creature. He wriggles about in the net from left to right and back again, trying to shift himself into a sitting position so he can get a better look. From nearby, Goldie lets out a squeal of terror while rushing at high speed to hide behind a tree, as if pursued by a three-metre high pineapple.

A hammock ape knuckle-walks across to Noah and releases him. It sniffs at his Chow suit, its expression full of curiosity. Noah stands up, keeping a cautious eye on the potentially ferocious creature.

The ape's commander clears her throat. 'Uh-hum. Are you going to introduce yourself, trespasser?'

103

Noah braves looking up. His amazement is such, his mouth opens and locks itself into an 'o' within his Chow headpiece. When he finds his tongue, all he can say is, 'Cool—that is so cool.'

'What is this "cool" you speak of? Are you insulting my colour with one of those bad-taste snow jokes?'

'Oh, no … no, no, no, I wouldn't dream of doing that. Cool means impressive—even excellent.'

'Is that so? Please excuse me for not returning the compliment. I find *Canis sapiens* a most disagreeable, unimpressive, and inferior species—especially one as woolly as you.'

The albino woman, who's more human than dog, light-foots off her albino male reindeer's saddle. Both woman and reindeer have the same shade of red eyes. The reindeer has a dense white pelt and huge antlers of metallic-grey. The woman has close-cropped white hair, a round face, and a small beak of a nose. She reminds Noah of a snowy owl. Around her neck hangs a necklace of trophies: feathers and other less desirable dried bits of things he would rather not know about. Her clothing consists of a white waistcoat, seemingly made out of hammock ape fur, underneath which she appears to be wearing a loose-fitting, dark-grey suede T-shirt and matching trousers.

'What you staring at, lion-face?' she asks. 'You want to end up in my larder?'

Noah sticks his tongue out at her.

Her face breaks into a grin, displaying a set of small and sharp teeth more suited to a rodent than to a woman. 'A boy in *my* forest? Where have you come from?'

'Finn McDrool brought us here to hide.'

'That stinking giant. Have you smelt his feet? He

could've asked me first.'

'Are you Phoebe Watson?'

'Depends on my mood. At the moment, I'm Professor P. Watson. But if you rid yourself of that ridiculous get-up, you can call me Phoebe.'

'Oh, that. Well, on one condition…'

She beetles her white eyebrows at him. 'You're in no position to offer me conditions, boy. I could still be a witch, you know, even if I haven't a wart on the end of my nose.'

'I'm Master N. Padgett, but you can call me Noah—only if you promise not to hurt Miss S. G. Golden Retriever, or any of my other friends.'

'That's two conditions. What other friends?'

'Lord H. MacScottish Terrier, Mr J. Whippet, Mr B. Bulldog, Miss M. Jack Russell, Miss T. Beagle, and Master P. Labrador.'

'Quite a bounty on you lot. Wonder what they'd pay me. Shame I ate six of them for breakfast.' Her expression is deadpan, the pupils of her eyes the colour of blood.

Noah breaks into a cold sweat inside his Chow suit. 'That's impossible.' Even as he says this, a part of him hovers on the edge of doubt. She might have the appearance of a human, but that doesn't mean she *is* human.

She points a finger at him. 'Your suit?'

He points a finger back at her. 'Your promise?'

Phoebe turns to her reindeer. 'What do you think, See-are-tea?'

The reindeer does a snorting huff.

'Well, lucky for you, Master Padgett, See-are-tea says "yes". And once you've removed that daft fur of yours, for crying out loud, do tell Miss Golden Retriever to come out of hiding. You never know, I might even help you find your friends.'

Without the suit's insulation, all that stands between Noah and the biting wind is a one-piece cotton undergarment. He wonders if Phoebe wants the weather to slay him, to save her the trouble of doing so. He stuffs the fun fur into his backpack and holds out a hand to Goldie.

She sidles over to him, trembling, with her eyes darting from left to right. 'Oh, Noah, are y-y-you qu-qu-quite sure about this?'

'Remember what Finn McDrool told us. As long as I stay looking like a boy, Phoebe won't harm us.'

'Might not have known you were a boy, but for your rudeness,' says Phoebe. 'I bet you never dreamt that sticking out that silly pink human tongue at your elders might save your life one day. Have you got anything to camouflage it with, before you hit the city?'

'How do you know I'm going to the city?'

'Time we get a move on,' she says, legging it up into the saddle on her reindeer's back.

'You've not answered my—'

'Stop talking. Stop asking questions. Just grab my hand.' She hoists him up, to sit in front of her.

'What about Goldie?'

'What about her?'

'I'm not coming, if she isn't.'

'Darned boy. Why slow yourself up with a shivering wreck for company?'

'Haven't you ever heard of friendship?'

'Not lately. But … oh, come on, then. Bring your friend, if you must.'

Soon the three of them have mounted See-are-tea: Phoebe at the front on the saddle as she's the heaviest (apparently reindeer have weaker backs than horses, hence the shoulder-saddle), Goldie in the middle, and Noah behind her. As they ride along, Noah learns why Father Christmas is never pictured riding on a reindeer; even a saint would be hard-pressed to stay jovial with a sharp, bony spine digging into his crotch.

At first, they travel at a gentle trot, but the deeper in the forest they go, the closer together the dial-oaks, so See-are-tea has to slow to a walk. Noah guesses they are nearing Phoebe's camp, when all the tree-faces start to resemble her. Also, the hammock apes here are obedient to her command to the point of comedy. She only needs to click her fingers at them and they scurry down the trees and line up on the ground: her soldiers awaiting orders. They in turn order the corkscrew ducks around, treating them as lower-ranking creatures. It is breakfast time just now, so the ducks have to wait for their superiors to take their pick of the fungi first.

See-are-tea comes to a stop and stands there, obviously thinking he has arrived at his destination. Noah cannot see anything other than trees, ducks, and apes.

Phoebe sticks two fingers in her mouth and lets out a whistle. Someone or something lowers a rope ladder from two-thirds of the way up a dial-oak. 'Follow me,' she says, shinning the ladder with the agility of a hammock ape.

Anyone who has ever tried following a person up a rope ladder will know it's a far worse experience than sharing a solid ladder with someone else. Added to this, there's Noah's total mistrust of ropes as a means of ascent, following on from his last bad experience in the school gymnasium. As he starts to climb, Phoebe's tree house gives the illusion of swaying about above him, even though he realises it's he and Goldie who are doing the swaying. For once, Noah is more frightened of something than his friend, who's behind him, promising to catch him if he slips.

Once Phoebe reaches the tree house, it becomes a clearer fixed point to aim for; not quite a house, he soon learns, but two dial-oaks joined to create a natural shelter out of their top branches in the shape of a Celtic roundhouse.

Safely arrived, Phoebe winds up the rope ladder after them.

Noah swivels his head about, trying to take it all in. 'Wow!'

'Amazing, isn't it?' says Phoebe, 'and all down to teamwork. The hammock apes did the reinforcing and weatherproofing of it. They used a mixture of pressed dial-oak leaves, hardened tree resin, their own excrement, and crushed corkscrew duck eggshells.'

Noah points to a log-burning stove in the centre of the room. 'Is that made of amber?' It looks out of place, if not too hi-tech for Phoebe's primitive home.

'It's the work of the reclusive arcanist, Terces Scimarec.'

'Oh, right … okay,' he says, without an idea in his head what she's talking about.

Goldie tugs at his sleeve and whispers in his ear. 'Ask her where our friends are.'

He clears his throat. 'Professor Watson, you seem to have broken your side of our agreement.'

'Postponed, not broken.'

'That's not fair.'

'Well, it'll just have to be. I have an earlier agreement to honour first.'

'What earlier agreement?'

'You'll have to wait for Finn to return from Aisalartsua.'

'So now you admit to having had some kind of arrangement with him all along? Well, I hope when he returns, he won't spend a whole week talking about his holiday and showing us boring photos of himself, instead of making himself useful.'

<><><>

Each time Noah sees the Zyx-dimension moon, it bothers him more than the time before. He can't help thinking it conceals something unpleasant beneath its surface.

'How can a lunar landscape have such a flawless surface?' he asks Phoebe.

'Exactly,' she says.

Noah is tired of Phoebe's obscure answers to everything he asks. He decides that either she has too high an IQ for the average person to understand, or she's insane, or she's a sneaky liar who conceals her underhanded behaviour in riddles.

He tests his hypothesis with a random question. 'Are you human?'

'I refuse to put my racial origin on application forms.' She closes her eyes and yawns.

'But that's not what I asked you.'

Keeping her eyes closed, she tosses the question back at him. 'Tell me, Noah, how would *you* feel about an application form which asked if you were human?'

'Uh-hm, let me think … well, back home, I'd think someone was taking the mickey. But in this dimension I'd fear a yes-answer might end badly for me.'

'Exactly, so don't ask me that question.'

'Okay, so is there anything I *can* ask you?'

'Not really.'

'Not, how old are you?'

'Definitely not that one.'

'What are you doing living in a forest all on your own?'

'Nor that one.'

'Why do you call yourself a professor when you don't have any students and don't like answering questions?'

'In my experience, Noah, those who keep asking questions are too busy talking to hear the answers. You really ought to polish up your listening skills—you'll need them around Percival Poodle.'

If Phoebe wanted to render him speechless, she'd just succeeded. Why had she suddenly mentioned Bluebell's abductor without prompting? What was the poodle-man to her?

She fixes upon him, her mouth twitching with amusement. 'Percival's idea of conversation is for him to do all the talking and for his listener to be enraptured by it. If you look bored for a moment, butt in, ask a question, or pass an opinion uninvited, you'll have lost all opportunity of rescuing Bluebell.'

Okay, so Finn McDrool has filled her in about Bluebell, but how would she know so much about the right way to behave around that thieving poodle?

'You have to trust me on this,' she says. 'It's essential for you to know this one thing—that however tedious, loud, or opinionated Percival becomes, just hold your tongue. If he does ask for your opinion, make it brief, and choose your words wisely. Provide him with no opportunity to twist what you're saying, as he'll trick you into digging your own pit and falling into it.'

'Has he ever made you fall into your own pit?'

'If he had, I doubt I'd be here to tell the tale. Take it

from me, if you don't learn the art of quiet counsel now, then, when you're under pressure later, you'll never put the brakes on your tongue before it proves fatal.'

<><><>

'Good to see you, me lad,' Finn says, sticking his lupine snout in Noah's face when he's attempting to take a nap.

Noah peers at him out of one eye. 'Your nose is peeling. Did you forget to pack your sun cream?'

'I was in a forest fire.'

'Horrid things, those.'

'Yes, horrid.'

'You m-m-must put on your s-s-suit, Noah,' says Goldie. 'Finn wants us to leave with him.'

'What about the others?'

'They're waiting for us elsewhere.'

'Where's Phoebe?'

'Vanished.'

'What do you mean, vanished?'

'One minute sitting here, next minute bright light, then vanished like a ghost.'

'Why would she vanish?'

'Work, she told me. She left behind some stuff for us to take on our journey. I've packed it for you.'

'What stuff?'

'No idea. Odd and ends. Some I've never seen before. She said you'd know what to do with them when the time was right.'

Noah puts on his fun fur and has a rummage in his backpack. Four bags of IEG sweets. An herbal body spray named *Cleenodre* claiming to 'deny the dog within'. A boxed board game called Trap, with purple and pale pink squares and a set of wooden chess dog-men. A bag of huge glittering marbles; one has a rainbow arcing through its middle. And right at the bottom of the bag, a

111

posh-looking black leather box.

He lifts the box out. It has the words *Messrs Glister and Sparkle of Dnob Street (Jewellers and Watchmakers)* embossed on it in gold letters. The inside of the box is lined with white-satin cushioning and contains a square gold watch with 'Percival Henri Oscar Louis Poodle' inscribed on its back.

'Finn, do you reckon this watch is stolen property?' he asks.

'No, it's custom-made and worth a mint.'

'Is Phoebe rich?'

'No, just well connected.'

'What if I get mugged?'

'You won't. Not wearing this over your fur.' Finn reaches inside his leather jerkin and hands him a roll of brown cloth. 'Here, put it on.'

Noah discovers it's a monk's robe, complete with a large hood and a rope-belt. 'Why would I want to wear this?'

'Folks tend to respect them holy types and leave them be.'

'But who do they worship?'

'Cosmo the Star-maker—not that I personally believe in him.'

'Is that what they call God, around here?'

'Who's God?'

'Cosmo the Star-maker, I suppose.'

112

CHAPTER ELEVEN

Cosmo the Star-maker and the Holy Order of Pugs

One whole week, ZDT, of travelling with Finn McDrool—mostly perched on his smelly shoulders—is not Noah's idea of a holiday. Dressed in his Chow suit with a monk's robe on top, Noah feels like an overheated potato in a fur-lined sack. For the sake of passers-by, he and Goldie are to pose as holy pilgrims, with a giant Irish Wolfhound-man as their chaperone.

They have just arrived at the top of Telgup Scarp. Across from them is Gup Beacon, which Finn says is three-hundred and four metres high. This makes it only one-metre off qualifying as a mountain. An old river meanders through a valley between beacon and scarp. From up high, the river reminds Noah of a sparkling water-serpent giving birth to crescent-shaped oxbow lakes. The monastery nestles at the foot of the beacon. It looks much too peaceful for Noah's liking: the sort of place where souls enter but never leave. Phoebe has left instructions that he wait there until further notice, without giving even a rough estimate of how long this will be.

He wants to hate everything about the monastery and its surroundings. Ever since his mum died, anything to do with quaint architecture or breathtaking scenery upsets him. He lets out a long sigh, followed by a deep shuddering inhalation as he thinks of all those houses and gardens they used to visit together, which always ended with a cream tea: just the two of them. She wanted to do this for him, as she'd never had the opportunity to do such things in her childhood.

Up on the scarp, the air smells fresh as clean laundry blowing on a washing-line in spring. Birds swoop and dive about the valley. Distant bells tinkle on gusts of wind. Despite himself, the moment is so perfect it makes him tingle from head-to-foot and brings happy-sad tears to his eyes.

Then he thinks of Bluebell.

So far, he has worked hard to parcel up his emotions and keep them buried, to stop him going mad with sadness. But the string of the parcel has just snapped and let out darkest grief. First his mum. Now his puppy. 'Why?' he asks out-loud, without being fully aware of having opened his mouth. 'Why now?'

'It's the thirteenth hour of the thirteenth month of the thirteenth-hundredth year,' says Finn, 'and destiny's brought you here on a triple thirteen.'

Noah shouts at him. 'What a load of superstitious rubbish. You haven't the foggiest about anything. You know nothing … hear me? Not one single thing, at all.'

'Set yourself down off me shoulder, Noah. Rant. Cry. Shake your fist at the sky. Tear up the grass. Beat me up, if you like. And when you're ready, we'll go where we're expected.'

114

Finn lets Goldie down from his other shoulder. She goes to lie on her side, propped up on one elbow with her head in her paw-hand, with a smiling, faraway expression on her face. 'If I were you, Noah, I wouldn't bother exhausting yourself with useless emotions. Best to practise sitting quietly, as the holy Pugs do.'

He snaps at her, not in the mood for anyone to preach to him. 'How would you know about the Pugs— or calmness, for that matter?'

'They came to me in a dream, promising to show me the art of inner peace. Then all my hair would grow back, they said.'

'And just how long will that take? Weeks? Months? Years?'

'Can't say until I try.'

'Well, it might help *you*, but it won't help Bluebell.'

'I think it might help her very well.'

'Can't imagine how.'

'If you'd ever seen me in full coat, you'd know what I had in mind.'

'I'm fed up with everyone talking in riddles. Just tell me straight.'

'Not when you're in such a surly mood.'

'Fair enough, and see if I care.'

'Have a biscuit, Noah,' says Finn, putting a hand in one of his pockets and pulling out something that looks suspiciously like a large grubby bone-shaped dog treat. 'Cheese, with a smidgen of chamomile and valerian to sedate yourself.'

Noah crosses his arms, frowns, pouts, and shakes his head firmly at Finn. The giant ignores him and chucks the biscuit in his own mouth, without bothering to wipe off the dirt.

Fixing his attention upon the monastery, Noah

115

counts twelve parsnip-shaped spires crowning a main building about the size of Westminster Abbey. It has a graveyard behind it and a large courtyard out front. A long single-story building with a kitchen garden stretches along the rear, as well as fourteen huts with allotments. The walls of all the buildings are made of the same pink brick, and the roofs of something resembling solar panels. A white-painted picket fence surrounds the complex.

'We'll start making our way down into the valley at fifteen-thirty hours and ten seconds,' says Finn. 'That'll mean we arrive too late for Fifteenth-hour Prayer, but in time for lunch.'

'That's fine by me.' Noah flops down on his back and closes his eyes, banishing all thoughts of Bluebell from his mind. He listens to the sounds around him, allowing them to soothe him. Insects buzzing. Larks trilling. Grasshoppers chirruping. Geese honking. Sheep bleating. Wind rustling the grass. A single bell rings, calling the Paters to Fifteenth-hour Prayer.

Struck by the mathematical impossibility of squeezing someone as ginormous as Finn into a building meant for normal-sized dog-people, Noah asks him. 'How will you fit in the canteen for lunch?'

'Not stopping, young fella. Going home. Done my bit. Cosmo the Star-maker will let the Paters know when the time is right for you to carry on.'

'And what if Cosmo the Star-maker doesn't let them know?'

'Then perhaps he'll let *you* know instead.'

'Great. So I could spend the rest of my life waiting on a sign from Cosmo the Star-maker.' Noah turns his back on Finn to watch clouds piling in and draw a darkening shadow over the valley. As the clouds

116

advance and eat up the sunlight, they remind him of the ones on his computer screen back home. He shudders at the sight of them. What if the clouds have come to reclaim him, and they return him to his dimension without Bluebell?

A rumble of thunder sounds in the far distance. He leaps to his feet, desperate to escape down the hill to shelter as fast as he can.

<><><>

A robed Pug-man glides over to greet them in the courtyard. Despite the incoming rain, his head is uncovered. He has dark-brown eyes, a mask-like flattened black snout, small black velvety ears, an apricot coloured head and neck, and looks quite young, despite all his wrinkles.

Finn says to him, 'I'll be leaving Master Chow and Miss Golden Retriever in your capable hands, Frater Tobias.' The giant squats down and pats Noah on the head. 'See you around sometime, young fella.'

'Don't go, pl…' Noah starts to say, but the giant has already stepped over the fence and begun to head up the valley before he can persuade him otherwise.

The storm gathers momentum, flashing and crashing about the sky as if Cosmo has hired a massive amount of strobe lighting and a full timpani section of an orchestra for the occasion. Tobias hurries them along into the reception area where he hands Goldie over to Miss Lydia Pug, who's employed to look after female visitors. Then he leads Noah to the guest-dormitory where there's a baggy T-shirt, pair of jeans, and a towel laid out on a bed in apparent readiness for his arrival. Tobias points out a wash area behind a wooden screen and leaves him in peace to clean up.

Not knowing how long he has, Noah dare not

117

remove his Chow suit for a decent wash. Instead, he sprays himself liberally with some of the *Cleenodre* body spray Phoebe put in his backpack. He's optimistic its floral stench will cover up any human smells coming off him.

Tobias reappears and takes him to the refectory. This is a dining room similar to the canteen at school, except its tables are longer with benches down either side. There's a strict rule of silence during mealtimes, which Noah thinks he'll have difficulty obeying. He has just spotted Goldie across the room, as well as Phil Labrador, Minnie Jack Russell, Bonzo Bulldog, Tamara Beagle, and Hamish MacScottish Terrier.

When they've greeted each other—miraculously without anyone uttering a word—they share a meal of gritty stoneground bread and a bowl of lumpy mushy-pea soup, followed by prunes and anaemic custard. Normally Noah would refuse to eat such food, but this is a reunion celebration.

Once they are out in the courtyard, Noah asks Phil, 'How did you lot get here?'

'Haven't the foggiest,' Phil replies, scratching himself behind the ear and gazing up at the retreating storm clouds above. 'It happened all in an instant—one second strung up by the hammock apes, and the next, this dump.'

'But why didn't Phoebe send us together?'

'It beats me, mate.'

After two whole months in the monastery, Noah concludes there's a plot to keep him from rescuing Bluebell. If not, everyone seems determined to delay things long enough for her to forget him. The pugs have assured him he can leave when he has finished helping them bottle an order for Healthful Brew, an herbal drink meant to make you look younger if you drink it regularly. Noah thinks this is sale's hype, considering there are some extremely wrinkly, grey-faced Pugs around the place, especially the Pater in Chief, Bartholomew Peregrinus.

Today, Bartholomew has invited him for an early morning stroll outside the monastery to watch sunrise. 'You can leave your Chow suit behind, if you like,' he says, as casually as telling him he doesn't need a sweater.

'I wondered when you'd notice,' Noah replies without fluster. Ever since his IEG sweet supply had dried up a fortnight ago, he'd expected someone to comment on his pink tongue.

As they walk along the riverbank, he notices the sky is more of a hodgepodge of colours than usual. It's as if Cosmo has mixed a new batch of paints on his artist's palette. There are greens, blues, yellows, oranges, purples, and pinks of various combinations and shades.

'It's a rare happening for both suns to rise at the same time,' says Bartholomew. 'Normally, there's half-an-hour to a couple of hours' difference between the two of them.'

They stand in silence for a while. Then, all at once, both suns float up and crown their respective horizons with brilliant liquid balls, one of fuchsia pink and the other of deepest crimson. Noah finds it such an awesome and dizzying sight, he throws himself down on his back in the dewy grass to stop him tipping over.

Above him, hangs the moon, undiminished in its whiteness despite the suns. 'Pater, why doesn't the moon have any hills or plains? And why is it so very white?'

119

'That's the way it is. But now I have a question for you, too. Why is Professor Phoebe Watson so white?'

'What's that woman got to do with this?' Noah's heart speeds up at the mention of her name. It seems everyone is involved in some kind of conspiracy, with him at its centre. He decides to play along with Bartholomew, to find out what he's driving at. 'She's an albino, of course.'

'Did you ask her why she's an albino?'

'No, that's rude. Anyway, I know the answer already.'

'Which is?'

'She was born that way, without skin pigment.'

'What would you say if I told you that Professor Watson hadn't always been an albino?'

'I'd say it was rubbish.'

'That's not a real moon up there, you know.'

'What is it then?'

'An artificial satellite disguised as a moon. It's called Vermis Porta One.'

'How come *you* know this, when everybody else thinks it's a proper moon? And since when have artificial satellites lit up the whole night sky?'

'I worked for the Government as a scientist, until Cosmo called me to Holy Orders.'

'Oh yeah? Funny, ha-ha!'

Bartholomew ignores, or chooses not to react to Noah's sarcasm. 'I stumbled upon the sacred writings of the ancient Niradnam race—'

'Which said?'

'That the Messengers of Cosmo travelled to the Zyx solar system and gathered together all the spare rocks floating around in space to construct a new heavenly sphere named Epacsranul.'

120

'Now you're confusing me. First you say the white moon is an artificial satellite called Vermis Porta One, and then you suggest it's a legendary thing made of rock by supernatural means.'

'About fifteen years ago the Government sponsored a space mission to the 'Moon', to find out if there was any life buried beneath its crust. But instead of discovering life, they found its centre was hollowed out to support a 'gravity well'. Without going into complicated science, this gravity well suddenly made inter-dimensional travel possible.'

Noah scents the first real clue to his being here. Maybe Bartholomew is not yarning, after all. 'What did the scientists do next?'

'The Government had them build a top secret laboratory in the moon, code name Vermis Porta One.'

'But if you'd stopped working for the Government by then, how would you know this?'

'I've friends in high places who go back a long way. They've visited me from time to time over the years. They trust me with their secrets.'

'Why are you telling me about it, then?'

'Because you're an innocent victim.'

'And Bluebell, too.'

'Yes, her as well.'

'Is there a Vermis Porta Two?'

'I couldn't say.'

<><><>

Five days on, Noah has decided Bartholomew is going out his way to avoid him rather than risk having further questions slung at him about the possibility of a Vermis Porta Two.

It is the first day of the week, not that it makes any difference to the routine. Noah avoids prayer, has breakfast, avoids more prayer, slouches about in the library for an hour or so, slopes off to the dormitory for a quick snooze, plays board games with Phil Labrador, and avoids more prayer.

After this, he sneaks into the kitchen garden with Jimmy Whippet and keeps watch while his friend steals some blackberries the size of fir-cones. Whilst they sit eating them, Frater Tobias comes along and tells them, 'No apple and blackberry pie with ice cream for lunch.'

'That's a joke,' says Jimmy. 'There ain't any ice cream in this place.'

They go and hang out in the main courtyard to enjoy the sun, but Frater Paul spots them lazing about and insists they help him and Frater Stephen shift crates of Healthful Brew from the storeroom to a lean-to near the front gate.

Following an hour or more of hard labour, Noah mutters under his breath, 'If you exist, Cosmo, get me out of this place.'

Immediately he says this, he's rewarded with a possible answer to his prayer: the clatter of horses' hooves, the rattle of empty long-carts, and the sound of Sergeant Salt yelling at the top of his voice.

'Oh no, I don't believe it,' says Jimmy, dumping the crate he's carrying and charging off so fast his tail escapes from the back of his trousers. Before he disappears through a door in the opposite direction from the kitchens, he calls back, 'I think I might've left the kettle on.'

Frater Stephen lets out an exasperated tut. 'That's not very helpful.'

'Never mind him,' says Frater Paul. 'We mustn't keep Salt waiting, or else…'

Noah counts, 'Nine crates left—that's three each.

I'll race you. See who shifts theirs first.'

By the time Salt and his mob have steered their four carts through the open gate, all the crates are neatly stacked in the lean-to, awaiting collection. The Sergeant leads in, wearing his three-cornered hat. He stands up on the front of his cart with his knees flexed and his feet wide apart. From this position, with the help of long reins and a great deal of swearing, he achieves control of two speckled grey mares hitched to the cart. Private Pegleg has stationed himself at the back, as far from Salt as possible.

On the second cart, Lance Corporal Watt fights to control a pair of frisky white horses, while Major Tom lounges about in his yellow jacket being useless.

Captain Mac follows, his cart pulled by black and white piebald horses. He wears his usual sky-blue jacket, with a full leather purse at his belt. Lance Corporal Dittle sits beside him, wearing a bored expression.

The last cart bears the deranged Lieutenant Stark, of the pink silk jacket and matching peak cap. He rides alone, doubtless for good reasons, his horses having to interpret his unintelligible grunts and a variety of rhythms tapped out on their rumps by his walking stick.

Private Pegleg yells across to Noah, 'Hey mutant … long time no see.'

Noah stands outside the lean-to with Phil, adopting a chilled out pose. The noise of the LIMS' arrival has drawn the rest of the gang to the courtyard: apart from Jimmy, of course.

'What's that mangy loudmouth's problem?' asks Phil.

'Lack of promotion opportunities, most likely.'

The carts are manoeuvred into a position easy for loading, side-by-side with their opened tailgates facing

123

the lean-to. Lance Corporals Watt and Dittle wipe the overheated horses down.

Major Tom wanders over to Stephen with a clipboard and pen. Through his monocle, he checks the consignment of Healthful Brew against his paperwork.

Sergeant Salt removes his hat and chucks it in the cart. He says to Lieutenant Stark, 'It don't hurt to show them holy pugs a bit of respect, just in case we need sheltering from aggro one day.'

'I thought *they* were the aggro that others needed sheltering from,' mutters Noah, convinced only Phil can hear him.

Salt's ears prick up. 'Watch your P's and Q's you little sprat.' He strides over, with a grin on his face, and gives Noah a hearty slap on the back. 'Perhaps you're not such a little sprat, now. What have them pugs been feeding you? You're tall enough to join the LIMS.'

Finding himself at eye-level with Salt, when previously he had been level with his neck, comes as a real shock to Noah. How many months is it? Is his next birthday about to pass him by, without his knowing it? 'Are you going to Nod Nol City?' he asks Salt.

'Maybe. Why do you ask?'

'Me and my friends need to come with you.'

'What's it worth?'

'My undying gratitude.'

'How many friends are we talking about?'

'Seven of us.'

'Seven cons on the run, risking the capital? You and them might as well stand in front of a "WANTED" poster and shout HERE WE IS!'

'We're a team.'

'The deal is for the LIMS to transport you, and no-one else.'

'That's not fair.'

'Ain't fair to you, or to the other six?'

'To us, as a group.'

'Are they your mates, or ain't they?'

'Of course they're my mates.'

'A bunny chaser, a digger, a roller, an all-fours romper, a biter, a scat-binger, and a double-crossing thief? That ain't a working army. You lot can have a knees-up when the job's done.'

Phil sticks his face a snout apart from Sergeant Salt. 'You've just called me an "all-fours romper"? I'm not a flipping crawler-pup. The "all-fours" is a super-cool move. You wanta see some of my street-dance moves, Sarge?'

'Nope, Master Labrador, I don't reckon I do.'

The rest of Noah's friends move in to have their say.

Lord Hamish clacks his teeth at the sergeant. 'Just who do you think you are?'

Bonzo wrinkles his face tight in a scowl. 'It's utterly absurd to dispense with my superior digging skills when there's a city to get in and out of.'

'And you'll need a scout to send along the tunnel once it's dug,' says Minnie.

Salt crosses his arms in front of his chest and nods at Goldie and Tamara. 'How about your two girlfriends over there? Ain't heard a squeak out of them.'

'Sorry, Noah,' says Goldie, looking at the ground. 'It's peaceful in this place and my hair has nearly grown back. Do you mind if I wait here for you?'

Her answer pricks at his heart like a thorn, but caring about someone means doing what is best for that person—whether canine, human, or some place in the middle—even if it involves a goodbye. Noah would

125

never forgive himself if Goldie was injured or killed on his account.

'What about you, Tamara?' he asks.

'I've developed rather a liking for the organic compost heap here. I'll stay here as long as they'll have me, then I'll check out the nunnery for compost.'

'What? No more foxes' poo ever?'

'It used to cause me stomach and skin problems.'

'Okay, I respect your decision, 'and yours too, Goldie.'

Salt doesn't appear to have noticed their conversation has finished. He gazes up at the sky, whistling a non-tune to himself. Noah cannot resist looking up, too, just in case he catches sight of an eagle, a flying saucer, or an asteroid. But there's nothing out of the ordinary there: just a cloudless blue.

After a minute or two more of scratching and gazing, the sergeant cups his paw-hands around his cavernous mouth and hollers, 'Jimmy Whippet—you rogue, you swindler, you miscreant, you foul wretch, you double-crossing swine…'

A door bangs from across the courtyard and out sidles Jimmy, his shoulders hunched and his eyes concentrated upon his feet. He stops outside the door and shuffles about on the spot.

Salt's grim face breaks into a grin. 'Come to Daddy.'

'You've got to be joking,' says Noah. 'Jimmy's your son!'

'*Step*son.'

'Why are you so rude to him?' What with his own negative experience of having a step-parent, Noah expects the opposite answer to the one Salt gives.

'Because I loves him, I do,' he says.

'So why is he hiding from you, then?' Noah asks, unwilling to accept this as the truth. Step-parents don't call their stepchildren all the rude names under the sun, as if they hate them, when underneath they love them, do they?

Salt explains, 'He nicked a heap of tinsel off me, and I dobbed him in to the old Bill.'

'But what's so bad about nicking tinsel? Why go to the police?'

'Tinsel, meaning sparkly stuff, meaning precious gems—you banana.'

'Did you, by any chance, steal those same gems off someone before Jimmy stole them off you?'

Salt taps his nose with his finger and says nothing.

Noah has an inspiration. 'Were you thinking of inviting your stepson along with us?'

'Nope.'

'That's a shame.'

'What's the pitiful scallywag's done to earn him an invite?'

'He's such an expert in breaking and entering.'

'Spot on. That's why I'm going to conscript him into the LIMS, instead of asking him nicely.'

Noah thinks this an excellent idea but, for the sake of his friendship with Jimmy, he asks, 'Is that fair?'

'If you want to half-inch your four-leg friend out from under that poncy poodle's snout, it is.'

'Her name's Bluebell.'

'Not any more. Take a gander at this.' Salt removes a crumpled piece of paper from his trouser pocket and hands it over.

With shaking hands, Noah unfolds and smooths out the glossy front cover of a monthly magazine titled *Prize Collectables*. Pictured there is a chocolate Labrador sitting on a fluffy cushion. She has on an emerald green collar studded with bling. Beneath her reads the caption **CHANTELLE: the latest addition to entrepreneur Percival Poodle's priceless collection of unique alien specimens.**

Phil lets out a huff of disapproval. 'He's a law unto himself. How's he get away with it? If it were me, or any other geezer behaving like him, they'd end up in the slammer or the nut house.'

'Difference between you and him,' says Salt, 'is he's top of the Rich List and you've got less than nothink.'

'But that dog looks far too grown-up for Bluebell,' says Noah.

'You ain't the only titch who can sprout round here.'

Whilst all the talking has been going on, Jimmy has snuck over and is hovering about behind his stepdad. Salt swings round and grabs him by the arm, keeping hold of him while yelling at Private Pegleg to fetch some equipment from the cart.

This equipment turns out to be a folded-up brown uniform, a backpack, a water canteen, and a packet of energy biscuits. Salt shoves the various items at Jimmy, whose eyes are watering with emotion—either sadness, anger, fear, or a bit of each. 'From now on in, Private Whippet,' says his unrepentant stepdad, 'you'll address me as "Sergeant" and do as I say, but not always as I do. Anythink you nick is mine, but you'll have a chance to earn it back, if I'm so minded.'

'But why must I join your stupid army,' asks Jimmy, 'when I'm happy to come along voluntarily for Noah's sake?'

'I need you thinking like a soldier. Our mission is to return the alien specimen, Chantelle, to her rightful owner. If we get this wrong, we could end up dead.'

'The name Chantelle stinks,' says Noah. 'She's Bluebell.'

'She's Chantelle, until I say otherwise.'

'But if we're whizzing in and out again, how will she come when I call her?'

'One: she's had the name Chantelle longer than the name Bluebell. Two: we ain't whizzing in and out, or sneaking about. And three: didn't I mention Percival Poodle's expecting you?'

— CHAPTER TWELVE —

Le Château Blanc et Somptueux

Welcome (not) to Nod Nol City, thinks Noah, a place cleaner than Switzerland (if that's possible) but more stinky than a chemical factory; body sprays, deodorants, eau de colognes, mouthwashes, floral disinfectants, air fresheners in abundance, each cancelling out the other's good qualities.

Salt has just told him off for sneezing, even though the sergeant can't stop sneezing himself. Added to this, Noah's eyes are watering profusely due to extreme glare. Dazzling whitewashed buildings with dazzling glass. Dazzling white marble. Glittering fountains. Pavements sparkling with quartz. Roads as straight and level as Roman ones in Ancient Britain, with bright white lines down their centres, sky-blue lines down their sides, and purple and white 'Arbez' crossings for pedestrians.

He points out some trees to Jimmy. 'Are those made of plastic?'

'Yep. And the flowers, too.'

'What about the grass?'

'Nylon.'

'Birds?'

'Feathered, plastic or nylon, you mean?'

'No, silly, I…'

Jimmy winks. 'Caught you! No birds, no wildlife, no nothink.'

No cars, buses, or youngsters playing in the street. No mobile phones ringing, bicycle bells, church bells, singing, personal stereos, or pets. Into this sterile cityscape explodes four carts stacked high with rattling crates, pulled by horses dispensing dung onto the pavements. The fact that nobody arrests the loudly cussing LIMS for causing public disorder and pollution, demonstrates just how much the citizens of Nod Nol hold Percival Poodle in awe.

'If the Poodle's expecting you,' Jimmy says to Noah for the trillionth time, 'I don't see the point of you wearing that Chow suit or having to call Bluebell "Chantelle".'

Noah shrugs his shoulders. 'Perhaps your stepdad's just winding me up.'

A troop of mongrel street-cleaners appear with shovels and poo sacks to clear away the horses' dung as fast as it falls. Some other dog-men, with crossbred terrier faces, ride on tricycles pulling trolleys. On the trolleys are containers of disinfectant, which the terrier-men squirt through hoses at the marks left behind on the road by the dung. Behind them walk official-looking spaniel-men with clipboards and magnifying glasses to check the job is complete.

Jimmy tells Noah that the Environmental Cleansing Team (ECT) had to do unpaid overtime for a month after the football cup's semi-final at the City Stadium. When Looprevil United beat Nod Nol City and local

131

supporters trashed the City, Percival Poodle—himself a football fanatic—ordered the law courts not to punish them.

From what Noah has learnt about Nod Nol City so far, he can't help thinking it is one vast joke: Percival's joke, at which nobody but the joker dares laugh.

The Poodle residence, Le Château Blanc et Somptueux, looms high above the city on an artificial hill.

Noah whistles through his teeth. 'Talk about showing off to the neighbours.'

'And snooping on them, too,' says Jimmy, with a mischievous chuckle. 'You see those buildings to the foot of the hill to the east? Those are the Law Courts, and to the west, the Government Offices.'

Noah cranes his neck to take in more of Percival's abode. The only uniform thing about it is its white exterior walls. Apart from this, it's a real hodgepodge of styles. It has steep copper roofs weathered to a soft green colour, dotted with little windows with gables. Numerous turrets and conical towers sprout upwards like different varieties of mushrooms. Some have battlements at the top and others have spires. The main windows are long, slim rectangles divided by vertical stripes. Every exterior door, whether it's one of the numerous single side doors or the main double doors, is set beneath arches and painted white.

Noah thinks the white doors look quite ridiculous; they remind him of something belonging to a fairytale palace in a cartoon. A baddie, such as Percival, should own solid oak doors that creak open and bang shut, as in Dracula films.

The residence disappears from view as the horses and carts reach the base of the hill and start to climb a

132

winding roadway up to the main gates. White flowering trees and shrubs grow on either side of the road in abundance. Noah notices their overbearing perfume, especially that of the everlasting magnolia. 'I thought you said all the trees and flowers were fakes around here,' he says to Jimmy.

'Only in the city. The poodle don't hack competition, that's all.'

They reach the hill's flat plateau, which is circled by a castle-like crenellated wall with additional barbed wire along its top. Major Tom's cart is the first to arrive at the white painted iron gates. Sergeant Salt's cart is fourth in line. Noah strains his ears to hear a conversation between the Major and two pit bull terrier security guards, but it's impossible to pick up what these guards are saying as one of them is chewing gum and the other is doing the macho gangster thing of not opening his mouth more than a millimetre to speak. They look as if they're dying to pick a fight just to give them a break from their boredom.

Lieutenant Stark, who's sitting on the cart in front of Noah, begins to drum an impatient rhythm with his walking stick on its wood. Sergeant Salt yells at Stark to shut the (something) up, and then fires off a round of obscenities at the security guards, one of whom points a gun at him.

Undaunted, Salt stands up on the cart and swears even louder at the guard. When the guard shows no sign of backing down, Salt adopts a quietly dangerous tone. 'If this-here cargo explodes in the sun from your delaying tactics, your boss will get you by the short and curlies and string you up.'

The electronic gate opens without further delay and a scruffy overweight mongrel, in leather-jerkin and

133

baggy trousers, lumbers into view. He gesticulates and gabbles so fast, his words turn into something like *u ou ear I air u y*. Noah thinks maybe Percival makes a habit of employing vocally-challenged staff, so no-one can argue with him. But Major Tom seems to know what the mongrel is on about, even managing to exchange some brief pleasantries with him about the weather.

Their carts pass by the front of the château and on down its left side, where they arrive at some double doors leading to Percival Poodle's cellars. A team of leather jerkin-clad, scruffy mongrels spill out of these doors and begin unloading the crates of Healthful Brew. They come over as a happier crowd than the cranky lot so far, bantering as they work, although their breaths stink like slimy harbour walls.

Noah mutters to Jimmy, 'Talk about rotten teeth. You'd think Percival would pay for them to go to the dentist, what with his obsession for cleanliness and sweet perfume.'

'Shush,' says Jimmy. 'Don't let anybody hear you calling him by his first name, or you'll end up in the dungeons.'

'He has dungeons?'

'So Pegleg says.'

'What should I call him, then?'

'Monsieur Poodle. And you must draw it out, so's it sounds all la-di-dah and nasal, stressing the second part of each word, like this... (Jimmy pinches the end of his snout with his paw-fingers) '...Moss-*your* Poo-*delle*.'

'Affected, or what? He's obviously never been to France. Bet his real name is Joe Bloggs from Putney.'

'What in Zyx's name are you talking about?'

'Oh, nothing in particular. Just muttering to myself.'

'I'd keep your muttering down, if I were you.'

'Well, you're not me.'

Jimmy winks at him. 'Wouldn't *want* to be you, neither, baldy-face.'

Noah doesn't feel in the mood for joking by now. He's overheating in his Chow suit, overdosing on IEG sweets, and his nerves are all a-jangle over how he's going to get to see Bluebell. Fear, excitement, impatience, and confusion all scramble about in his brain at once, so his head threatens to explode. He takes a few deep breaths, but even these stifle him. Closing his eyes, he attempts to think of nothing, but the thoughts just keep coming, harder and faster. Opening his eyes again, he searches for anything to divert him from his stress.

The carts are parked on a wide gravel drive with an herbaceous border of white flowers and shrubs alongside. Past the herbaceous border, a path leads to the rear of the château, where there's a vast lawn cut in neat stripes all going in one direction. On the far side of this lawn is an avenue of huge trees; sweet chestnuts, he guesses from their greyish trunks and white-flowered catkins.

Oh, for some proper colours, he thinks. No sooner has he wished for this, than he glimpses a flash of colour and catches sight of a youthful-looking, reddish-gold Labrador-man leaping headlong into a shrubbery. It happens so fast, he wonders if it's his imagination. Certainly no security alarms are sounding, or guards thundering across the lawn. Perhaps the Labrador-man is one of the château's employees practising stunts on his days off, or maybe Percival Poodle employs some ex-Roomdaorb patients.

Jimmy Whippet interrupts his train of thought, not

seeming to have noticed anything out of the ordinary. 'They've finished unloading. Time for a treat.'

'What treat?'

'Some spiffing nosh, my good fellow.' Jimmy sticks his snout in the air, playing the snoot. 'Canapés on the terrace and a spot of uncorked Healthful Brew served with glacé cherries and slices of lemons on cocktail sticks.'

'You're not serious, are you?'

'Just mimicking Percival when he's sober.'

'What's he sound like when he's drunk, then?'

'Like my stepdad.'

'Will we have cheese and pineapple on sticks?' Noah is thinking of a cocktail party Kate once held, when she wore a sparkly dress and shoes with crippling heels. And a load of stupid gits came along, with bad smells under their noses and nothing interesting to say, so they all bored each other to tears within minutes. He reckoned they were only there for the free sparkly wine and had no intention of seeing each other again. The women were all on diets and the men on heart pills, which gave him the chance to scoff a whole plate of vintage cheddar and pineapple on sticks, followed by a mountain of expensive chocolates. He nearly threw up afterwards, but it was worth it.

'Come off it, Noah.' Jimmy gives him a friendly cuff around the ear. 'As far as that jumped up Poodle's concerned, we're a load of nobodies. If we're lucky, we'll get given squirrel pie and chips, with a drink of smart-save squash.'

<><><>

Noah stares down at a plate of brown rat-tail bolognaise, his stomach screwed in such a knot, he's afraid it will rupture. An armed security guard is standing less than

136

two metres away with his dark glasses trained upon him. As Noah continues to sit there, awaiting commencement of his force-feeding by the guard, a sound reaches him from somewhere upstairs in the château. He does his best not to react, despite exploding with excitement inside. To help ease the pressure, he pretends a sudden itch has afflicted him on his back that needs scratching.

The muffled bark repeats itself, unmistakably belonging to Bluebell although deeper than he remembers. The security guard removes his dark glasses and smirks at him. Noah masterminds a blank face and braves a mouthful of bolognaise. It doesn't taste as bad as he expected. He chews it up, swallows it and says, for the guard's benefit, 'Yum—tasty.'

'You can have mine, too, if you like,' says Captain Mac, pushing his plate across the table to him, his bolognaise untouched. 'My stomach's too delicate for anything other than rabbit.'

'Yeah, right,' says Noah. The captain has never said more than two words to him before, and isn't to be trusted.

Mac grins at him. 'Don't worry. You can escape further culinary torture, if you like. I've an errand to run. …You coming?'

'Is that a question or an order?'

'Either. Both. Up to you.'

'Like I believe you're giving me a choice.'

'Depends if you want to see Chantelle now, or later.'

Noah's heart thumps so hard, it almost punches the rat-tails up out of his stomach again. '*That* name—'

'Shush!'

'Okay, so what's the errand?'

The Captain fishes a bundle of empty pull-string

purses from out of his jacket pocket. 'Money business and a personal request from Monsieur to you. He has a particular predilection for Chow-boys.'

'A *pre-dil*-what?'

Mac grins at him, his bright red gums a disconcerting contrast to his sleek black fur. 'A special, special, special liking for them, that's what I mean.'

'Can I take my backpack? I've some things for Monsieur.'

'Ah, some stuff from the albino witch. Surprise, surprise.'

'How do y—'

'No more chat. Just walk. I've got to check some sums in my head.'

The captain does his calculations aloud all the way down a long corridor, stopping only as he and Noah reach a lift. The door to the lift slides open, without him pressing a button, and a security guard waits inside to escort them up to Percival's apartment. The lift has mirrored walls; it ascends without a sound. Noah holds his breath and stares down at his feet. Neither Mac nor the guard speaks. He remembers too late that he hasn't had an IEG sweet after his mouthful of rat-tail bolognaise, and to think that Jimmy went to all that trouble nicking a new supply of sweets for him from the monastery kitchen.

His stomach shrinks further in on itself and his heart offsets its acceleration by skipping beats. If only he hadn't wished so hard to be free of Kate. This is his entire fault. Some sort of inter-dimensional ogre must have read his thoughts, answered his wish, and is now about to deliver him into the hands of someone a million times worse than his stepmother.

This should be the moment when he undoes his

wish and reverses time. In an ideal universe, the time would start the day before his mother died, so he could puncture her car tyres to prevent her going on that fatal journey. But then he would never have known Bluebell and it was impossible to imagine having her wiped from his history.

He could at least wish for a predictable existence in which he wakes up in the morning knowing what he'll eat for breakfast and what lessons he'll have at school that day. And in the evening, he takes Bluebell out for a walk in the park, eats his supper in front of the telly watching *The Simpsons*, does his homework, plays on the computer, and goes to bed, having had Kate tell him off at least a hundred times in the last twenty-four hours.

— CHAPTER THIRTEEN —

Doing Business with Monsieur

The pit-bull-man security guard presses the intercom to Percival Poodle's private apartments. There's a gold lion's head knocker on the door that probably makes a most impressive noise if banged, but Noah isn't in the mood to test it out. Above the knocker, is a gold nameplate on which the words 'Monsieur Percival, H. O. L. Poodle CDU, RFD, SNAW' are engraved.

'What do those letters stand for?' Noah whispers to Mac.

The captain puts a finger to his mouth and shakes his head at him.

A voice comes over the intercom. 'It stands for Coolest Dude in the Universe, Richest Fellow in the Dimension, and Someone Not to Argue With.'

'How did he hear me?' Noah mouths.

The voice comes again. 'Genetically enhanced hearing combined with superior technology.'

'Is this some kind of joke?' Noah doesn't bother keeping the noise down this time.

'X-ray eyes combined with superior technology,' says the voice.

Noah crosses his arms and seals his lips. *I don't believe you.*

'Oh, believe you me, it's true. …Amazing what money can buy.'

'You can mind-read?'

'I've not had that upgrade to my software yet.'

Amusement flickers across the security guard's granite face. 'That's enough of talking to the boss's door. Time to go inside and meet Monsieur Poodle himself.'

'That wasn't your boss talking, then?'

The security guard shrugs his shoulders. 'Follow me.'

The speaking door clicks and whirs open.

Ahead of them lies a white-carpeted corridor longer than in any stately home. Black and white photos of Percival Poodle line the walls on either side. Noah's legs ache with tension. Sweat drenches him inside his Chow suit. A nerve twitches in his right eyelid.

The corridor has no door at the end but leads straight into a white room as large as a gymnasium. The room has no furniture, other than at its centre where there's a vast glass-topped desk the size of a table-tennis table with a fibre-optic lamp on it and a crystal glass ashtray littered with squashed-down cigar butts. Percival sits facing the window, away from Noah. He's slouched in a white leather chair with his white patent leather cowboy boots up on the desk. Thick smog surrounds him; it smells like expensive cigar.

Noah fights to quash his disappointment at Bluebell not being in the room.

Percival lets out an affected high-pitched cough, followed by an equally affected yawn. 'I will be with you

141

in a jiffy, when I have finished meditating on matters of lofty concern.'

What a plummy and camp voice he has, thinks Noah.

The entrance door snitches on him again, this time through an intercom on Percival's desk. 'That Chow kid thinks you sound like Frolster Gimble.'

'Frolster Gimble, indeed,' mutters Monsieur. He starts to tap his claws on his desk in an unfriendly manner.

'Who's Frolster Gimble?' Noah mouths to Mac.

'He's a game show host, a miniature poodle with purple hair,' the captain mouths back.

The Poodle still has his back to them, which unnerves Noah far more than if he could see his face. His claw-tapping has turned to a fast drumming with the flat of his paw-hand, making him sound more insane even than Lieutenant Stark. This is accompanied by smoke billowing up in the sort of dense cloud that you would expect over an exploded noxious chemical plant.

With a sudden flourish, he removes his cigar from his mouth and grinds it into his ashtray as if he's grinding Noah's head instead. Then he smacks his paw-hand down on the desk so hard that the fibre-optic lamp teeters and slides a few centimetres nearer to the edge of the glass-top. 'Did you recognise that rhythm, kiddo?' he asks.

Noah fights a lump in his throat the size of a golf-ball. 'Um, are you talking to me, Moss-your Poo-delle?'

Monsieur swivels his chair around. His velvet emerald-green suit matches his *un*dog-like eyes. He shows Noah something halfway between a smile and a snarl. His teeth are very white and regular, as if he wore a brace as a pup-boy. He looks like a distant relative of

Denis on the Shopping Channel, whose daytime show Kate worshipped.

Thinking of Denis with all his velvet-lined jewellery boxes, reminds Noah of what he's carrying in his backpack. 'I've a present for—'

'The rhythm?' He tilts his chin and raises his eyebrows.

'It slips my mind just now, Moss-your.'

'That is, if it was ever in your mind, kiddo.'

He gives Noah such a long, hard stare it makes the sweat inside his Chow suit evaporate.

'While the Captain and I are busy conducting our business, perhaps you would like to meet Chantelle? I take it you know who Chantelle is?'

Noah's heart rate almost goes off the Richter scale. He fights to keep his voice level. 'Yes, Moss-your, I've seen you on telly with her.'

'Yes, of course, you would have seen her, wouldn't you?' He leans back in his chair and rests his head in one of his paw-hands, with his elbow on an armrest. With the other paw-hand—upon which he wears an oversized signet ring—he clicks his paw-fingers at the security guard. 'Darren, show Master Chow to the playroom, would you? Make sure Chantelle has her favourite ball, so they can have a bit of fun together while we finish up here.'

Noah glances at Captain Mac, who offers him an indulgent smile. He has seen that look before, on the faces of adults who like to forget they were ever children themselves. It says 'I must be nice to the brat, but can't wait to see the back of him'.

Darren places a paw-hand under Noah's arm and guides him across the room.

As they are about to exit via a side door, Percival

calls out, 'By the way, the rhythm belonged to "Dupe it, snare it, anyway you want it"—one of my old favourites!' He lets out a high-pitched snarling chuckle, the type unhinged hillbillies do when they are about to torture something or somebody. 'See you in a while, crocodile.'

Now he turns his attention to his wristwatch, glaring at it, tapping at it, and holding it up to his left ear. 'Darn it, if my watch isn't broken. Never mind, perhaps a most timely replacement is lurking in a certain little Chow's luggage?' He tears off his dead watch and tosses it into the waste bin next to his desk. From where Noah's standing, it looks alarmingly similar to the square watch Phoebe gave him.

The security guard tightens his hold and propels Noah through the door.

'Challenge you to a game of Trap after tea!' Percival yells after him, letting out a yodel of delight.

<><><>

Noah walks next to Darren, occasionally having to break into some faster steps to keep up with him. It's yet another leg-achingly long corridor, this time paved with large limestone squares rather than carpet. It has huge picture windows down its right side and numbered doors down its left. As they pass the first door—No. 11—Noah thinks of the British Prime Minister at 10, Downing Street and asks Darren if Monsieur Poodle's office has the same number.

'Yep,' he says.

'What happens in No. 11?'

'Sums.'

Noah stops for a moment to look out of the windows. Beneath him lie the rooftops of some stark white buildings peppered with square windows. An emerald-green flag, at full mast, with a picture of Percival on it, flutters on a pole atop the highest and most central of them. 'What are those buildings?'

'Offices.'

'Whose offices?'

'Mr Percival's.'

'What does Monsieur do in them?'

'Governs.'

'Governs who?'

'The Government.'

'Yeah. Right.' Noah wants to ask if that's democratic, but he suspects Darren might not know what *democratic* means. 'What number is the playroom?'

'Sixty-five.'

'How long will I be allowed to spend with Blue … Chantelle?' *Whoops! Nearly slipped up there*.

'Shut up.'

'Okay.'

They descend a short flight of stairs and turn left into a windowless corridor with numbered doors on each side: odds on the left (starting with 51) and evens on the right (starting with 52). Noah thinks of the 'alien' museum in Area 51 at Roswell and wonders if the numbering is coincidental.

Giddy with nervous excitement, he counts in his head the odd numbers to keep himself earthed.

53, 55: Seeing Bluebell, after all this time.

57: Is he about to find himself trapped with her forever?

59, 61, 63: Both of them alien specimens in the château of a mad dictator.

65…

The door has an ordinary handle and no complicated entry code or key, indicating Bluebell isn't a prisoner but just a pet dog shut in a room for a while.

145

Darren puts his hand on the door-handle and an excitable woofing, clattering, and thumping starts up on the other side. The door shakes in its frame, reminding Noah there's a young adult dog rather than a puppy there.

'Shut-it,' shouts Darren, barging his way into the room past a vertically leaping loon pretending it's a rocket ship rather than a chocolate Labrador. She greets the security guard as if she likes him, especially when he produces a biscuit out of his pocket. When she has calmed down, he pats her on the head. 'There's a good four-leg. Who's a pretty girl, then? …Chantelle, my lovely sweetie-pie.'

Up until now, Darren has shown himself a pit-bull-man of few words and of little emotion, but with Bluebell he displays a different side altogether. Noah's feelings about this are mixed. Bluebell really seems to like the security guard, which is good because it shows he has treated her well, but bad as it means she has bonded with at least one of her captors. Worse still, while this love scene is going on between them, she's totally ignoring him.

Noah fights to convince himself this display of affection is between *Chantelle* and Darren, not Bluebell and Darren, but he knows his reasoning is flawed. The majority of Labradors don't suffer from split personalities and are very balanced dogs. This means they respond positively to anyone who speaks to them nicely, plus they show added enthusiasm towards anyone with a biscuit in his pocket.

With Bluebell at his heels, Darren picks his way across the toy-scattered floor of the large playroom. He scoops a soft squeaky ball from off a fluffy rug. The ball is black with blue spots, and the rug is emerald-green to

146

match her collar. He chucks the ball at Noah. 'Play!'

Bluebell dashes over to Noah, eager for a game, and then skids to a halt. She sits there looking puzzled with question-mark eyebrows, cocked ears, and her head on one side.

'Throw,' says Darren.

Noah tosses the ball to Bluebell, but she lets it fly past her and just stays staring up at him. He points his Chow paw-finger across the room at it. 'Go. Get your ball.'

When Bluebell hears his voice, she throws herself at him, knocks him to the ground, and lays into his Chow suit—half-fun, half-serious—just as she used to do with her bedding-fleece but with quadruple the strength.

Darren calls to her. 'Ball. Come. Good girl.'

'It's okay,' Noah says, while trying to wrest the Chow suit from her. 'I don't mind. She'll calm down in a second.' But Bluebell does the exact opposite of this, her excitement growing with every word he speaks.

Darren turns to leave. 'The door's unlocked. When you're sick of Chantelle, go to Room 51. Wait for me. And don't touch the monkey.'

Noah doesn't ask the security guard what he means about the monkey, as he wants him out of there, quick.

As Darren opens the door, a rending tear comes from the Chow suit. Darren stops in his tracks. 'What was that?'

Noah has to think fast. 'Whoops, pardon … trouble with wind.'

'Humph.' Darren frowns and scratches at his forehead. He looks as though the cogs of his brain are running slow and need rewinding. 'Rat-tail bolognaise,' he says, and carries on out of the room, closing the door behind him.

147

<><><>

Once the sound of Darren's departing footfalls has disappeared up the corridor, Noah throws back the headpiece belonging to the Chow suit. He squats down and Bluebell rushes into his open arms, treating him to a complete face wash with her rubbery pink tongue.

'Hello, Bluebell. You *do* remember me, then.' Tears of relief and joy moisten his eyes.

Hearing her name, she dissolves into a squiggly, tail-wagging, chocolate fur-ball of love. She concludes her celebration by dashing at high speed around the room at least twenty times with her tail between her legs and her ears flying behind her.

After this, she flops down panting and rolls on her back for a tummy rub. Then it's time for a game of tug-of-war with a square of blanket: a game that Noah used to win, just occasionally. But now she's so strong and the grip of her jaw so vice-like, he's forced to admit defeat after only a minute of trying; either that, or have his arms pulled out of their sockets.

As he sits on the floor, regaining his breath, he hears the approaching clickety-click-squeak of Darren's boots. Bluebell rushes to the door in excitement and springboards off it repeatedly, blocking the security guard's entrance in. This buys Noah enough time to sort himself out and look like a Chow once more. He tucks his T-shirt into his trousers to hide the tear in the side of his fun fur a moment before Darren barges in.

'You've over-excited her.' The security guard scowls at him.

'We played, like you said.'

He points a paw-finger at Noah. 'Watch your mouth.'

'Okay.'

148

'The Boss has invited you to lunch.'

'Can Chantelle come?'

'She always has lunch with the Boss.'

'That's nice. What are we eating for lunch?'

'Veggie-stuff.'

'What veggie-stuff?'

'Shut it. You're a headache.'

Darren goes out of the door again. Noah follows, with Bluebell running alongside nibbling playfully at his Chow-paw. They turn right and head up a couple of flights of stairs to a roof garden with crenellated walls around it. In the middle of the garden, amongst sub-tropical foliage in stone pots, sits Percival Poodle at the end of a white table that's at least two-and-a-half metres long and one-and-a-half metres wide. He speaks to Bluebell first, 'Ah, there you are, Chantelle. Come here, now. There's a good girl.'

She slinks rather than walks towards him, her head held low.

Percival pats her on the head and she jumps up onto one of the chairs to sit at the table, keeping a wary eye on him. He gestures to Noah with a sweep of his paw-hand. 'Come, sit down, kiddo.'

Noah plonks himself in front of the only other place setting, which is at the far end of the table from Percival. 'My name's Noah, not kiddo.' Annoyance swells inside him, itching to get out.

'And mine is Moss-your Poo-delle, so do not forget it.'

Noah makes sure to scrape his chair extra loud on the paved floor as he pulls it up to the table.

'Behave yourself, Noah Padgett,' Percival snaps at him. 'If you do not, I will have you sent to Room 51 for a cooling off.'

Noah inwardly gasps, shudders, and manages not to ask the first question that comes to mind. Instead he asks the second one. 'What's in Room 51 other than a monkey?'

'It is an ape, not a monkey. Everybody just calls it a monkey, out of ignorance.'

'Shouldn't apes live out of doors, so they can swing from trees and eat bananas?'

'Bananas are perishable.'

'What's wrong with that?'

'They are banned by Law—*my* law.'

'I know the trees and plants down in the city are plastic, but why can't you grow bananas on your own hillside?'

'They are yellow. That is why.'

'Not when they're peeled.'

Percival flashes his white teeth at Noah, in an approximation of a grin. 'Now who is a banana? How could I possibly grow peeled bananas on a tree? And if I could, how would I stop them turning black?'

'You could spray them with lemon juice.'

Percival's grin fades. He leans back in his chair and starts tapping a claw on the table. Bluebell whines and fidgets on her chair, as if she wants to make herself scarce but dare not.

'Shut it, mutt, or else,' he warns her.

She freezes, tightening her body up in an attempt to become smaller. It reminds Noah of what she used to do during one of Kate's temper tantrums.

'You're frightening her,' Noah says.

Percival bangs his paw-hand down on the table. 'But obviously I am not frightening you.'

'Actually, you are. But this isn't about me. You shouldn't scare dogs. It can make them turn nasty and

150

bite you.' Noah can't quite believe his bravery, or maybe foolishness in ignoring all the advice Phoebe gave him about not being mouthy around Percival. But the Poodle is even more of a threat to Bluebell than Kate was—Kate whom he should have stood up to better.

'Point one: I am the only one in the dimension who can utter the word "dog". Point two: Chantelle is not a dog. She is an alien four-leg. And point three ...ah, lunch at last!'

A Boxer-dog-man appears, pushing a silver trolley and dressed as a butler in a charcoal-grey coat with tails, striped trousers, white shirt, and bowtie. He has arrived via a lift, which Noah has only just noticed; a tall palm-like plant with spiky leaves blocks out his view of its doors.

Percival claps his paw-hands together in childlike glee. 'Ah, Seveej, there you are. I could eat an entire forest of chestnuts.'

'Yes, Moss-your. Very good, Moss-your. I hope chestnut bake is to your liking.' Seveej places a covered solid silver plate in front of Percival. He lifts the lid from it. In the middle of the plate is a portion of food that looks like a miniature veggie-burger swimming in a sea of white sauce. Percival inhales the steam rising from his lunch in an affected manner.

Seveej serves an identical meal to Noah on an ordinary white china plate. Noah's stomach growls in protest, his growing body demanding food, but his insides tied up in such a knot that the mini portion on offer seems a mercy. To go with this small mercy is a choice of vegetables, none of which he likes: parsnips, turnips, leeks with the green tops cut off, and new potatoes.

Having accepted only new potatoes, Noah asks

151

Percival, 'Do you only eat whitish food?'

'No talking until after I have said Ecarg.'

The butler brings Bluebell a bowl of what looks like cooked diced breast of chicken, rice, and turnips. As she inches forward in her seat, Percival holds up a warning paw-hand at her. 'Chantelle … Ecarg!'

The butler mixes a cocktail for Percival that consists of some milky white liquid into which he squirts something from a flask the size of a vanilla essence bottle. He tops this up with Healthful Brew and decorates it with rice-paper bows on a cocktail stick. Noah has a tall glass of simple Healthful Brew, and Bluebell a bowl of water. Seveej wheels the trolley off a small distance, where he stations himself like a sentry.

Percival raises both hands, palms upward in the air and says Ecarg, which turns out to be a reverse of Grace. 'Cosmo, creator of the stars, thank you for my good looks and my genius mind, for my stealth and my wealth, for my power and my bought friends who would otherwise be my enemies, and for sweet chestnut trees with their white flowers. Please forgive chestnuts their brown skins before they are peeled, and Noah Padgett for talking too much, and Chantelle for whining at table while thinking about biting me. Lastly, I ask you, Cosmo, creator of the stars, if you will cure me of indigestion and the extreme mental anguish it causes, so I do not have to eat chestnuts every day to keep my symptoms under control. So be it.'

If Noah was not so gobsmacked by Percival's prayer to Cosmo, he would have doubled up laughing. Instead, he feels slight pity for the fellow, adding to his hatred of him. He watches Percival pick up his knife and fork, then, with extreme concentration, cut up his chestnut roast into tiny squares and his vegetables into

152

tiny rounds, semi-circles, or ovals. After this, he forks up one piece each of chestnut roast and individual vegetables, which he takes slowly to his mouth. Once the food is inside his mouth, he chews on it at least thirty times, repeating the ritual with every mouthful.

So intrigued is Noah by the Poodle's obsessive way of eating, he forgets to do any eating himself.

After an eternity, involving only one-eighth of his first course, Percival looks up from his meal. 'It is rude to stare. Eat up, or your food will get cold.'

Noah polishes off the contents of his plate in about as much time as it takes Percival to eat three more mouthfuls.

Percival smiles at him in a fatherly manner. 'In my days at the Stock Exchange, before I made my first million, I used to live off doughnuts and strong coffee. If lunch ever happened, it consisted of tasteless sandwiches gobbled down in front of the computer. That is why I have ended up with ugly insides that don't match my good looks.'

'Your old life sounds like my dad's.'

'Do you like your dad?'

'Sometimes.'

'Perhaps you might learn to like me sometimes, then.'

'I doubt I'll be with you long enough for that.'

Percival returns to eating.

Bluebell has polished off her bowl of food and had a drink of water. When Noah catches her eye, she thumps her tail at him but stays sitting at the table with amazing self-control.

Eventually, Percival puts down his knife and fork. The meal has taken so long that the roof garden is no longer in the partial shade of earlier, but in full sun.

The butler clears away their dirty dishes and cutlery. He serves a portion each of honey cake and white rice-milk custard in identical dessert bowls to Percival, Noah, and Bluebell.

The poodle-man starts to put a mouthful of cake and custard in his mouth but then puts his spoon down again. He scratches himself behind his ear and gazes up at the sky, as if absorbed in some abstract thought or other. 'Noah,' he says, addressing the sky, 'what with this heat and the messy potential of custard, do you not think you would be better off without that silly suit on?'

The blood drains from Noah's face in a cold prickling rush, and he starts to upend like a ship running aground, keel first, on a high rock. He slings back his Chow headpiece to grab at some extra air and stop himself fainting. Bluebell squiggles around on her bottom on the chair, barely able to contain her excitement at seeing his face again. 'How long have you known about me, Monsieur?'

'Since Dr Jason Cairn recorded your birth. You won't recall him, of course, but you'll probably remember his wife, who is a Ward Sister at Roomdaorb Hospital. You were born underwater in a birthing-pool exactly on the dot of midnight. It coincided with a thunderstorm knocking out the hospital power for two minutes.'

'Why didn't my mum or dad ever tell me this?'

'They won't remember. It's blank-blank-blankety-blank—two minutes of Earth-time missing from their lives.'

'You've been watching me throughout my life so far? That's creepy.'

'No. My good friend Phoebe Watson has watched you, and others.'

154

Noah's heart does a backflip and misses a few beats. *Phoebe? His good friend? He's got to be joking.* 'Are there other children here, too? Are they coming soon? Why am I here? It's like alien abduction. You're not going to do experiments on Bluebell or me, are you?'

'The Professor is right. You are a nosy little chatterbox. By the way, who is Bluebell?'

Noah had assumed that Percival knew everything, so there was no point in keeping up the whole 'Chantelle' thing. *But what if he doesn't know there's a connection between Bluebell and me? And if so, why not?* Noah tests this theory with a white lie followed by a truth. 'Bluebell is my imaginary friend. I'm an only child, you see.'

'Yes, I was an only child, too. My imaginary friend was called Gertrude.'

Noah fights to keep the corners of his mouth level. 'What did Gertrude look like?'

'Like you—off-white and mostly bald, apart from the hair on her head. She wore an emerald-green dress with matching shoes.'

Noah changes tack, hoping to catch Percival off-guard whilst on the subject of friends. 'How do you know Professor Watson?'

He extends a paw-palm to Noah, a dangerous glint in his eyes. 'My watch, if you please?'

With speed, Noah reaches under the table for his backpack. 'Sorry, so sorry. Thanks for the reminder.' His hands are shaking as he rummages about amongst loose IEG sweets, an empty can of *Cleenodre*, spare clothes, discarded energy bar wrappers, and escaped carved dog-faced Trap pieces. 'Would you like some marbles to be getting on with?'

Percival starts to tap his claws on the table. 'Are

155

you calling me insane?'

'I don't mean those sorts of marbles. I mean these. They're really nice … real collectors' pieces.'

He snatches the marble-bag from Noah and peers inside it with suspicion, as if its contents might come alive. 'Professor Watson never mentioned these.'

'Well, she put them in my backpack, so I assume they're meant for you. You're the one that's a collector of priceless treasures, not me.'

Percival chuckles to himself and holds up the rainbow marble to the light. 'This is rather fine, if not rare. Yes, indeed it is.' Laying it down on the table with extreme care, he gets out one marble after another, remarking about the rarity of each. When the bag is empty, he turns his attention to arranging the marbles into ranks to form a triangle. He points to the largest one on its own at the front, which is emerald-green and glittery. 'This one is me.' Then he points to the smaller, less showy ones in the back row, 'and these are the ones that will never be me.'

By now, Noah has emptied out his entire backpack on the table but still can't find the watch. He feels all around the inside seams, re-checks for hidden zips and compartments, pats the lining, in case there's a tear in it and the watch has slipped in between. …Nothing. He's well and truly dead.

'My watch,' says Percival.

Noah turns the backpack inside out, wishing he could shrink down and disappear into it.

Percival lets out a high-pitched giggle. On the table, behind his rank of marbles, sits an open, empty velvet-lined box. He puts his wrist to his ear, to listen to the new watch he's wearing. 'Tick-tock, tick-tock, tick-tock.'

'How did you manage to pull that stunt?'

'You must know your friend Jimmy Whippet has light fingers?'

'You mean my *ex*-friend.'

Percival scoops his marbles into their bag and snaps the jewellery-box shut. 'Please excuse me. I have to carry out an inspection of the Government Offices.'

'And what about me?'

'You can help Darren take Chantelle for a walk around the grounds, if you like, and I will see you again at teatime.'

<><><>

Although a prisoner in this place, it soon becomes clear to Noah that its members of staff are under orders to treat him well and not stare at him as if he's a freak. Having had his Chow suit confiscated from him, his only option is to wear what his host has provided: jogging trousers with an emerald-green stripe down the outside of each leg and a white T-shirt with 'P.H.O.L.P is the GREATEST' printed on it in emerald-green. P.H.O.L.P stands for Percival Henri Oscar Louis Poodle. The fact that everything fits Noah exactly, including the brand-new white trainers, is too creepy for him to consider in depth.

The security guards go about their duties with cold military precision, except for Darren, who proves better company, even if sparing in conversation. As the pair of them walk past the entrance to the cellars, it's clear that Major Tom and the gang have departed the château, as their horses and carts have gone.

Off the lead, Bluebell makes mad dashes amongst the shrubs and around the lawn. Noah can't help smiling at seeing her so happy. He guesses his imprisonment with her is better than imprisonment without her. When she does her business in the middle of the grass, Darren clears it up with a green poo-bag and deposits it into some kind of stinky pit in the ground with an iron lid to it. 'Compost,' he says.

Bluebell returns to Noah at intervals, and runs along next to him, nibbling at his fingers, looking up at him, laughing in a doggy-sort of way.

'I think the Boss's favourite creature likes you,' comments Darren. This is the first complete sentence Noah has heard from him.

'Does Monsieur have any other creatures?'

'What? Apart from you?'

'I'm a human boy, not a creature.'

Darren seems to find this amusing. He doesn't exactly laugh, but his expression lightens. 'Monsieur is a collector.'

'Am I part of his collection?'

Darren looks up at the sky and starts whistling a tune.

They arrive at the avenue of sweet chestnut trees. Halfway down the avenue, they pass a young Labrador gardener going in the opposite direction, pushing a wheelbarrow with a couple of bags of manure, a fork, and a rake in it. He wears a wide-brimmed green sun hat, large dark-green-tinted sunglasses, and a green-checked shirt with plain green trousers. 'How you doing, mate?' the gardener asks Darren.

'I'm good.'

'And your friend?'

'He's Noah. Belongs to the Boss.'

'That's cool.'

'How's the routine?'

'That's cool, too, mate.'

Noah has no idea what the two of them are on about, but the word 'mate' combined with 'cool' sets

158

him wondering. Bluebell wanders up to the gardener and has a sniff of his green wellie-boots. The gardener squats down and gives her a brisk rub, making her go all squiggly and silly. He then looks up at Noah. 'A little birdie told me she likes carrots. Growing some whites for her, special. The boss would never have orange ones in his veggie garden. An okay idea, innit?' He stands up and exchanges a high-five with Noah. 'See you later, alligator!'

As the gardener goes on his way, Noah fights to contain himself from leaping about punching the air, until he does his maths. 'Darren, how long has the gardener worked here?'

'On and off.'

'On and off? Days? Months? Years?'

'What's it to you?'

'Just interested.'

'He and the Boss go back a long way.'

'What do you mean?'

Darren taps the side of his snout with a finger. 'None of your business, unless the Boss decides otherwise.'

159

CHAPTER FOURTEEN

Checkmate

T he dining room has chandeliers hanging from the ceiling and a view overlooking the Law Courts. Tea consists of cottage-cheese sandwiches, clover-honey and double cream on white scones, vanilla-iced shortbread biscuits, white-chocolate and chestnut muffins, and a drink of milk. Percival insists Noah tries something of everything, and, despite the knot in his stomach, Noah can't resist seconds of the shortbread and the muffins. Bluebell has crunchy off-white biscuits soaked in milk, and licks her bowl clean until it sparkles.

Percival seems in a good mood, so Noah risks starting a conversation. 'I met someone really nice today. He was doing your garden. Darren says you've known him a long time.'

'Did Darren tell you anything else?'

'No, he doesn't say much.'

'That's because he is well trained.'

'What's the gardener's name?'

'Philippe Labrador. Why? What is so interesting about him?'

'I liked him.'

'We were patients together at Roomdaorb, many moons ago.' Percival chuckles to himself. He doesn't look in the least embarrassed or ashamed at admitting he was an inmate in a hospital for the criminally insane. 'Philippe is a repeat offender, whereas I was only sent there for correction once. During that time, I made a couple of life-altering decisions.'

'What were they?'

'Number one, I vowed to deny the dog within, big-style.' Percival leans back in his chair, turns his eyes heavenward, and starts singing an out-of-tune version of a song Noah recognises from Private Pegleg's zPod.

'And two?' Noah asks, anxious to give his eardrums a rest.

Percival jumps up from the table and bounds to the window. 'Is it not obvious? He gives an expansive sweep of the paw-hand. 'Can you not see the huge success I have made of myself—too huge, even, for the Law to touch me. In fact, I have *become* the Law.'

Noah has never met anyone with such an inflated ego. He longs to accuse him of behaving like a dictator without any true friends but thinks it safer to butter him up. 'Moss-your Poo-delle, you're quite astounding.'

Percival puffs out his chest like a vain turkey cock. 'Thank you, Noah.'

'I'd love to hear how you got sent to Roomdaorb.'

He grins as wide as a shark. 'I trashed Nod Nol Central Library ... broke in at night and ripped up every last book.'

'What made you do that?'

'A teacher called Miss Freda Basenji once called me "thick" in front of the whole class.'

'That's very rude. Where I come from, she'd have been suspended or sacked from her job for that.'

161

'I am really intelligent. Much more intelligent than Miss Basenji was.'

'Why did she say it?'

'I had difficulty reading and writing, so all the letters got jumbled up on the page. It runs in my family.'

Noah guesses Percival is talking about dyslexia. He tells him, 'I know of someone who was allowed to take his university exams on his laptop.'

Percival looks puzzled. 'How is that easier than a table?'

'Don't you have laptop computers in this dimension?'

'No, only tabletop or portable ones.'

'Do you have a computer?'

'No. I have a phone.'

'Why can't you have both?'

'Because I prefer a decent shout.'

'But you *can* shout at a computer. For instance, if it crashes before you've saved some important work you've just done, or you lose a game on—'

'That reminds me. It is time for our game of Trap.' Percival claps his paw-hands together in excitement.

Noah tightens up, wondering if all the pieces are there in the bottom of his backpack.

From a patch of sun under the window, Bluebell flicks the end of her tail at him, as if to say *I still love you, Noah, even if the rest of the world is about to turn against you.*

Fighting for calm, Noah says to Percival, 'The box has come undone. Do you mind if I empty out my bag on the table to find all the bits?'

Percival gives a bored wave. 'Get on with it then.'

Noah tips everything out, forgetting about his IEG sweets, which roll off the table onto the floor. Bluebell leaps up in excitement and starts dashing around the room, racing him for them. Noah apologises to Percival, 'Sorry, sorry … didn't mean to.' The poodle-man doesn't look in the least amused and starts to drum his paw-fingers on the table in extreme agitation.

When Noah has retrieved the last of the sweets, he steers Bluebell back to her patch of sun. 'Good girl. Now, lie down, Bl…Chantelle.'

'I do wish you would pronounce her name properly,' says Percival. 'It is Chantelle, not *Bleh*chantelle.'

'Yes, Moss-your. Sorry.'

'Oh, do stop apologising. It is very tedious. I expect you to entertain me, not to creep to me like all the other sycophants around here.'

This triggers a memory in Noah. It's of him sitting in front of the computer, surfing the net ten minutes before Bluebell hit 'enter'. He was reading somebody's website. They had written about sycophants plaguing celebrities, hoping to gain advantage for themselves by hanging out with the rich and famous. Sycophants operated in Ancient Rome, too, by attempting to curry favour by acting as informers. This often backfired on them so they ended up dead.

But there is something more to this. It's not just Percival's use of the word 'sycophant'. What is it? Noah racks his brain. *Yes, that's it—the link* **www.zyx-dimension.com** *had flashed up on his screen. It had appeared like one of those pop-ups:* **'Congratulations: you are the 1000th visitor to this site. You are the winner'.**

Percival pats his mouth to stifle a yawn. 'Do snap out of your daydreaming, Noah. Look, the board is still in the box. Hand it over here.' He spends the next few minutes attempting to line up the board's sides parallel with the sides of the table. 'You know, as far as gifts go,

163

I am not very satisfied with this. Some of the rows of squares are not squares at all.' He jabs a paw-hand claw at an offending row. 'Look at this lot. The ranks are too close together, while the files are too wide.'

Noah has to do some quick thinking to avoid punishment for someone else's bad craftmanship, or crafts*dog*manship. 'Perhaps it's handmade … unique … extra valuable.'

'Maybe, but I'd have preferred its creator to have used a ruler. How are you getting on finding those pieces?'

'Not sure. I could put them on the board and see, if you like.'

'No, give them to me.'

'Okay.'

'I insist on being purple. Always purple. If you hate pink, that is your problem.'

'No, I'm cool with pink.' Noah scratches his head, confused. Why purple? He'd thought white and emerald-green were the only acceptable colours around here.

Percival starts to line up his pieces into their sets, each one exactly in the centre of its square and facing precisely forward.

Noah holds his breath for seconds at a time, not daring to interrupt him, willing none of the pieces lost, yet powerless to alter the outcome: that of three empty purple squares and two empty pink squares crying out for their occupants.

'Stop messing about,' says Percival, holding out a paw-palm for the missing pieces. 'Hand over *my* three purple infantrymen, or else. And whilst you are at it, how about *your* pink high priest and warrior, too?'

'The craftsman ran out of wood.'

'Liar! Professor Watson would have fed the fellow

to a tree for lunch, for a lesser sin.' He stares at Noah, as if challenging him to a duel of untruths.

Noah averts his eyes from Percival to study the Trap-board and compare it to Chess. *Infantrymen instead of pawns. High priests instead of bishops. Warriors instead of knights.* 'You know, Monsieur, my two missing pieces are far more important to me, than your lost infantrymen are to you. Couldn't we play without them?'

'What? And later have it claimed that I only won the game because my opponent had a heavier handicap than I did?'

'I could use some of my sweets as infantrymen, and a screwed-up energy-bar wrapper as a warrior, and the top of my toothpaste tube as a high priest.'

'Better than nothing, I suppose. But you are not to mark my board with toothpaste or sticky crumbs, and those infantrymen must not roll off the table.'

While Percival gives his full attention to positioning the substitute items on the board, Bluebell pads over to Noah and puts her chin on his lap for a stroke. He fondles her ears and strokes her face, afraid he might not get the chance again.

<><><>

By nature, Noah isn't a competitive person. He prefers to use his above average, twenty points off genius intelligence to practise the noble art of laziness. This is why he can't understand his sudden fatal desire to thrash Percival at Trap. He has just given up his two marquesses, leaving him and his opponent five pieces each on the board, including their emperors. Fair and equal. Then Noah sacrifices his consort...

Percival leaps up from the table and claps his hands together in glee. 'Foolish Noah. Why throw away the

165

game with such abandon? Are you afraid to win?'

'Not at all, Monsieur. I'm declaring checkmate.'

'Stop messing about,' says Percival. He examines the layout of the pieces, talking himself through what has just happened, until his triumphant grin shrinks down into a hard line either side of his snout.

Noah feels sick; there's a taste of soured vanilla in his mouth. He can't take back his declaration, as it would involve returning his marquesses and consort to the board. Instead, he must blazon it through: his two warriors and one high priest, to Percival's consort, two marquesses, and one high priest.

Percival's voice comes out as a low growl. '*Grrr?* Yours are only minor pieces, compared to mine. *Grrr-Grrr-Grrr.*' He sweeps the pieces off the board with his paw-hand, grinds them into the floor underfoot, and picks up the board, breaking it in two. His skin shows through purplish-red beneath his single layer of fur. He opens his mouth so wide to holler for Darren, his tonsils turn purplish-red, too. Then he breaks into a fit of swearing a million times worse than anything Sergeant Salt would have come up with, and with all attempts at sounding posh forgotten. Noah is convinced something will burst in the poodle-man's brain if he keeps this up.

The security guard's approach sets walls trembling and doors shaking. He pounds along corridors and crashes through rooms, but doesn't risk entering his boss's dining room without first stopping to knock.

Percival clenches his paw-fists and hammers his own sides. 'Get in here, and stop your pussy footing.'

'What's the problem, Moss-your?' asks Darren.

Percival points an accusatory claw at Noah. 'Him is the trouble.'

'What's he done?' The security guard looks down at

166

the ground-up Trap pieces and the broken board on the floor. 'Whoops!'

'Whoops, you say? What kind of girly response do you think that is? Understatement of the year, or what? He cheated. Nicked some of me pieces when me back were turned.'

'Yes Moss-your, you never lose. Must have cheated. Bad Noah.'

Percival turns his back on them both and strides over to the window. He stands there clenching and unclenching his paw-fists. Noah freezes rigid with fear. Darren doesn't move a muscle, apart from casting a fleeting look of pity in Noah's direction.

When Percival swivels around, Noah jumps in terror. 'Under the circumstances, I think Room 51 is just the ticket.' Percival's voice is smooth but his smile like cut glass.

'Are you sure, Moss-you?' asks Darren. 'Think how much you've paid for your latest specimen.'

'I am not talking about Noah. He might be a naughty little cheat, but I can converse with him. He asks me intelligent questions and enjoys hearing me talk about myself.'

Darren's jaw drops. 'Oh no, you can't be serious?'

'Of course I am serious. Noah likes her and it will teach him a lesson.'

Percival leans under the table. 'Cooey, Chantelle. Room 51. Cage. Bread and water. Delightful companions. You will relish being the odd one out.'

'Don't—no, you can't.' Noah throws himself down on his knees and holds his hands up in an attitude of prayer. 'She hasn't done anything wrong. Send me. Please, please, please.'

Percival rattles his teeth at him. 'Shut up, Noah.

167

She is going, and *that* is that.'

<><><>

In Noah's reckoning, the bedroom is of identical size to his one back home. He wonders what to make of this: whether it's coincidence, intention, destiny, or an inter-dimensional quirk. Certainly its low ceiling and sky-blue walls are at odds with the high ceilings and white paintwork throughout the rest of the château.

On the wall facing the bed there's a huge framed portrait of the poodle-man, which makes Noah feel like puking. He thinks of the comedy movie in which Mr Bean destroys the priceless portrait of 'Whistler's Mother' with snot and paint thinner. If only he could do the same to Percival's picture, without it rebounding on Bluebell.

Lying down on his bed, he closes his eyes. What else is there to do, without any computer, iPod, or books to help him pass the time? What if Percival intends to keep him there for years in solitary confinement? The hours tick by, his terrors tumbling about in his head until exhaustion does him a favour and brings on sleep.

He reawakens in the midst of a dream, convinced some noise has disturbed him, yet finding everything locked in utter silence as if Cosmo has hit a universal pause button. The moon is high in the sky, framed by the window, frozen in time and space: that is how it looks, anyway. Then Cosmo hits the play button and Noah finds himself leaping about the room, punching the air in excitement.

From inside the château, he hears Bluebell let out a series of robust barks. Then from the distance—possibly beyond the city—come some answering barks.

<><><>

In the morning, Darren appears. He escorts Noah to the

168

'teliot' and back again to his bedroom. Noah tries to engage him in conversation, but to no avail. The security guard has a face of granite, and his vocabulary is composed of single-word responses.

'How long am I going to have to stay in here?' Noah asks.

'Dunno.'

'Will the ape hurt Chantelle?'

'Nope.'

'When will the Boss let her out of the room?'

He shrugs his shoulders.

Noah perseveres. 'He *will* let her out, won't he, especially if I promise to be good?'

'Dunno.'

'It's against basic human rights to deprive me of food and drink for this long.'

'So?'

'Wouldn't Moss-your prefer to keep me alive, considering my unique value as a collector's specimen?'

'Shut up.'

'Ah, two words. We're getting somewhere.'

He moves towards Noah with a raised paw-fist. 'I told you to shut up. Are you deaf, or somethink?'

Noah flinches from him, expecting a punch in the jaw.

Darren comes up closer and mouths to him *the room's bugged.* Having shared this piece of information, he starts shouting again. 'Stop your jabbering. Stop asking questions. Just blimming well shut it, if you want things to get better.'

<><><>

For the next three days, a mute Darren brings him regular white meals: semolina, anaemic bread, mayonnaise, white chocolate, and coconut milk. These

169

leave Noah bloated and lethargic, his condition not helped by lack of exercise.

Two nights ago, Bluebell had barked again and, as before, she'd received a barked response from far off. Then last night she'd howled like a werewolf and gained a howling reply from nearby in the city.

This morning, someone other than Darren brings Noah his breakfast. She's white with black spots and introduces herself as 'Room Service'. The last time Noah saw her, she was called Dorothy Dalmatian.

Handing him his tray of instant oats and coconut milk, she winks at him and says, 'I'll be back to collect your tray and to clean your room later, young sir.'

<><><>

A week into Noah's imprisonment, Dorothy serves him an extra-delicious breakfast of hot buttered crumpets with white clover honey and a glass of full-cream vanilla-flavoured milkshake. She reappears shortly after with a big white bath towel and a clean set of clothes and tells him he's free to take himself off for a decent wash in the bathroom (turn right out of his bedroom and last door on the left at the end of the corridor).

'What do I do after that?' he asks.

'Back to your room and wait for me. Then you can come and help me with my housework.'

He hates housework, but it's better than staying put another day.

His trip to the bathroom is total bliss. With a week's worth of grime to soak off, he hopes to stay clean for the rest of his life, however long that is. The bath is almost the size of a miniature swimming pool in the centre of the floor, filled with hot water and soap bubbles smelling just like his dad's body-spray. On its ledge sits a giant sponge, luxury crème wash, shampoo, conditioner,

170

nailbrush, and clippers.

After his bath, he brushes his teeth with a white toothbrush and white mint toothpaste, and combs his hair, now grown down past his shoulders.

Back in his bedroom, he finds a clean set of clothes identical to the previous set: an emerald green 'P.H.O.L.P' T-shirt and white with emerald-green stripe tracksuit bottoms. Dressed, he wanders over to the bedroom window, expecting everything to look the same as yesterday, and the day before, and the day before that. But a giant emerald-green and white-striped marquee has sprouted upon the lawn, and bunting (small strips of cloth like little flags on strings) decorate the place. At the moment, some dog-men are busy hanging lights along the row of sweet chestnut trees, while others are assembling some sort of sound system in the shade of the trees.

The gardener, Phil Labrador, sees him standing at the window, and smiles and waves to him. Noah waves back without smiling, unsure if Phil is one-hundred percent trustworthy.

Dorothy breezes into the bedroom, wheeling a trolley similar to the one belonging to Noah's school janitor. It's full of cleaning equipment such as mops, brushes, dusters, cloths, a bucket, fly spray, disinfectant etc.

As they walk down the corridor together, Noah asks, 'What's the occasion?'

'Monsieur Poodle's birthday party.'

'Am I going to be allowed to go to it?'

'Depends.'

'On what?'

'What happens between now and this afternoon.'

'Which room are we going to clean first?'

171

'The Boss' office.'

'Is he in there?'

'Not on his birthday. Either he'll be outside shouting at everybody, or doing a spot of wine tasting in the cellars.'

'He's having a day off Healthful Brew, then?'

'Let's put it this way. You won't want to be around him late tonight or tomorrow, if you can help it.'

'How do you know so much about him?'

'I've worked here before.'

'Same as the gardener, you mean?'

Dorothy lets out a quiet and playful woof in reply.

They arrive at Percival's office to find it spotless even before they start cleaning it. Dorothy explains that Percival has a phobia of germs lurking in dust, meaning he expects his office wiped down three times daily with a damp cloth.

When they've finished, they head out of the office, bypassing Room 11 without checking it out. According to Dorothy, Percival mistrusts recently discharged Roomdaorb Hospital patients around money: especially ones, such as herself, who've spent time in solitary confinement.

'Which room now?' he asks.

Dorothy whips an electronic key card out of her overall pocket. 'Guess?'

'I've no idea.'

'You want to see Bluebell?'

'Are you serious? Of course, I do.' Whilst saying this, a little voice niggles at him in his head. *Why is Dorothy here in the château? Why does she have a key card to Room 51? Whose side is she on? Am I being tricked? Is she party to a birthday joke? Does Percival want me out of the way for the day, shut in a room without windows?*

172

'Come on,' Dorothy urges him. 'I'm not meant to have this key card. A mutual friend of ours got it done for me.'

'Jimmy, you mean?'

Dorothy lets out another playful woof, which he takes as meaning yes.

'That scoundrel nearly got me into trouble over a wristwatch,' Noah says.

'He's just a bit of a chancer like his stepdad, Sergeant S.'

'Doesn't a chancer work for whoever will pay him the most?'

'Quite, which is why he's now in the employ of Graham Labrador.'

'What? The same Graham who lives in a shack in the woods and hunts for his food?'

'Yeah, the same. He might enjoy the simple life now, but only after making a fortune in the diamond trade—enough to retire early and have plenty left over to donate to worthy causes.'

Noah allows this piece of information to sink in, warmed by a glimmer of hope.

Outside the door of Room 51, Dorothy lets out a couple of short barks and Bluebell replies from the other side of the door. Dorothy swipes the card in the door entry system and pushes her trolley into the room, in case someone chances upon it in the corridor.

Bluebell rushes at Noah, knocking over Dorothy's bucket with a loud clatter and skidding about in its spilled soapy water. Whilst Dorothy wipes up the mess, Bluebell lets off some steam, kidnapping a broom from the trolley for a drag about the room and then giving a chamois-leather a good shaking.

Noah takes in his surroundings with horror and a

grim realisation of Room 51's purpose. *Poor, poor, Bluebell. A whole week in this tomb of a place, with freakish white creatures for company.* Amidst the sick collection, stands the ferocious-looking snaggle-toothed ape that Darren called a monkey. It might have been lethal in its day, but now it's stone-dead, its fists poised to hammer its great chest for all eternity.

Forty or so other glassy-eyed exhibits stare out of reinforced glass cases. None of them are easily identifiable as bird, mammal, fish, crustacean, insect, or anything Noah has ever seen or read about in books. There's a two-legged creature with a fat bulbous body, no neck, and a head with eight tentacles coming out of it; a snake with a parrot's head; and a millipede wearing a fixed grin on its flat face and standing on its rear end so it's the height of a full-grown man.

There are also two creatures Noah *does* recognise: a corkscrew duck and a basset-faced hammock-ape devoid of spots. Their presence here confirms Phoebe Watson's involvement in what should amount to an illegal trade if it weren't for Percival considering himself above the law. 'W-w-what is this p-place?'

'It's a private museum, of sorts.'

'That's not good enough. Tell me why they're here.'

'They're Percival's discarded toys—the ones he's got bored with.'

A shiver passes down Noah's spine. Bluebell stops playing and comes to lean against his legs, reaching up to give his fingers a lick. He chokes back tears, unable to deal with her trust and affection. 'Is this what he intends to do to Bluebell?'

'Not today,' says Dorothy, 'but we need to get her out of here whilst the going's good. And you, too.'

'You mean he might do it to us both?'

'Tomorrow maybe, after he has his latest specimen delivered to him—that is, if he likes it better than he likes you two. And this probably depends upon if his supplier has managed to get hold of another creature without 'bleaching' it in the process.'

'Bleaching it? What do you mean? Do you know what the latest specimen is?'

'No idea.'

'How do you know it's coming then?'

'About a fortnight ago Jimmy spotted the moon turning emerald-green for a couple of seconds. It does this whenever something new arrives, then there's normally a week of haggling over the specimen's price and a further week to ship it here.'

'So, Percival is a collector of alien creatures?'

'To put it simply, yes.'

'And he regards me and Bluebell as aliens?'

'Yes.'

'That means we're stuffed in more ways than one, if we're not out of here like yesterday.'

'That's about it.'

'So, what are we waiting for?'

'Percival's party to start.'

CHAPTER FIFTEEN

A Quartet of Wasps and Champagne on Ice

Darren sticks Noah on a raised platform next to Percival. Dignitaries file past and stare up at the poodle-man's prize exhibit. Noah squeezes a fake smile on to his face, while hating everybody in sight. All he can think of is Bluebell, still locked in Room 51. What if Dorothy fails to free her, as promised? What if he and Bluebell are still in the château this evening and Percival has rejected them in favour of his latest toy? He imagines his shiny dog beneath the taxidermist's knife and then entombed in a glass-case.

'Speak your mind, young fellow.'

Noah stares blankly, only half-registering someone is speaking to him.

The aristocratic basset hound-man, clothed in military uniform, barks at him, commanding a response. 'What's troubling you? Come on, spit it out.'

Noah snaps back at him, 'Why should I? I don't know you.'

'Haven't you ever met a complete stranger on

public transport and told him your life story?'

'Where I come from, we're told not to talk to strangers.'

'How extraordinarily rude. Why, in St Fido's name, would you wish to do that?'

'Fido is a stupid name for a saint.'

The basset hound-man adjusts the position of his half-moon spectacles to fix his droopy, red-rimmed eyes upon Noah. 'He's the saint of hospitality to strangers.'

'That's nice. I suppose.'

'Oh dear, you are a glum one.'

'You could say that.'

'I *have* just said it. Now, if you could overcome your reticence of talking to strangers, perhaps you would like to join me for tea on the terrace.'

'Monsieur won't like it.'

'Of course he will … won't you Percival, old fellow?' He clicks his heels together, to get the poodle-man's attention. 'How could anyone possibly object to General Reginald Basset taking tea with young Master Padgett?'

Percival is busy flirting with a strawberry-blonde beauty in a green satin ball-gown and a diamond tiara. He gives a dismissive wave of the hand. 'Go on then, if you want to be driven up the wall by a chatterbox.'

The General leads Noah out of Percival's earshot. 'So you *do* like talking, then? Or was Monsieur being sarcastic?'

'At first, I purposely asked Monsieur Poodle loads of questions to annoy him. But since I beat him at Trap a week ago, we haven't seen much of each other.'

The basset hound-man's dewlaps wobble with glee. 'You beat him at Trap! Well done, young fellow.'

They take their seats at a table for two. The General

177

removes his khaki cap. He pours out some exceedingly milky tea from a white-china pot into two white-china cups. 'You know how it is? Monsieur bans so-called "white tea" from his home, as it isn't genuinely white.' He forces some white-iced cupcakes and emerald-green marzipan fruits upon Noah, to go with his anaemic drink.

Noah nibbles at the offerings without appetite, while contemplating Percival's sham of a birthday party. He decides that if the poodle lost his money tomorrow, all his so-called friends would desert him. And the creditors would take all his possessions, probably including Bluebell in a glass case, and she'd end up dumped in some lock-up or put up to auction. At this thought, tears erupt from his eyes.

'Oh dear me, you poor young lad.' General Basset removes a neatly folded khaki handkerchief from his pocket. He shakes it out and hands it to Noah.

'It's alright. I'm okay. I'm fine. I can use my napkin.' Noah is furious at himself for blubbering in public like a baby.

'Good. I want you to look at the princess.'

'What?'

'The princess, if you please, but don't stare too hard.'

'Why should I look at a stupid princess?'

'In the name of Cosmo, you do ask too many questions. If you did that on the battlefield, you'd end up with a bullet in your head.'

'Is she the one Monsieur's drooling over?'

'That's the one.'

Percival is on a garden bench opposite Noah's table. The princess is sitting next to him, shading herself from the sun with a green and white striped parasol, masking

178

her face in shadow. On a low table next to the bench, there's an open bottle of champagne on ice. Seveej, the butler, stands at-the-ready to top up the fluted glasses belonging to Percival and the princess as required.

'Who is she?' Noah asks.

'Her Royal Highness Princess Suzanna of Nod Nol City.'

'And why should I find her interesting?'

'Just watch her and be patient.'

Several minutes pass, bringing Noah no nearer to sussing out what the General is going on about. Then a wasp singles Percival out and starts buzzing around his face. He attempts to shoo the stripy menace away but this revs the wasp up and makes it buzz ten times louder and swoop at him with venomous intent. Leaping up from the bench and erupting into one of his rages, Percival flails his arms around and beats at the wasp so hard, it has no option but to sting him on the neck.

Percival lets out howls of pain, punctuated by loud sobs and bad language. While the butler attends to calming his master, the princess peers out from beneath her parasol at Noah. Their eyes meet. At first he doesn't recognise her; then she smiles and it dawns on him he is looking at Goldie in her natural, full-coated glory.

<><><>

Three more wasps home in on Percival, all as obsessed with buzzing around his face as the first one. Seveej suggests using insect spray on them, but Darren says it might kill Percival if he inhales the stuff.

'I know how to make wasps go away,' Noah tells the General, remembering something useful his grandmother once told him—hopefully not one of her old-wives' tales.

'You're not thinking of helping that apology for a

179

dog-being, are you?'

'I need to take a closer look at the princess. She looks nice.'

'She's slightly highly strung at times, but you already know that, don't you?'

Noah leaves the question unanswered.

'Go on, then,' says the General. 'Save your enemy, if you must, and I'll watch your back.'

Before he loses courage and gives too much thought as to whether he can trust the General to watch his back or not, Noah hurries across to where the drama is taking place. He stops a short distance from Monsieur and clears his throat. 'Moss-your, may I offer a suggestion?' But it seems the poodle-man is in too much of a state to hear him.

Darren draws Noah aside. 'Not a good idea just now. Pass it by me instead.'

'He needs to calm down. Stop flapping his arms around.'

'Try telling him that.'

'I was about to, but you stopped me.'

Goldie catches Noah's eye briefly. Her mouth twitches at its corners and she lets out a cross between a laugh and a hiccough.

'Moss-your,' Noah calls out to him louder than the first time, 'you must listen to me.'

He stops flapping his arms around and his mouth falls open, almost letting in one of the wasps. 'You, Noah, ordering me ... *must* listen ... brat ... slice you ... I'll kill—'

Noah sidesteps Darren, as he makes a grab at him. He's determined to have his say. 'Moss-your, it's to do with your pheromones.'

'My pheromones!' shrieks Percival. 'How dare you

show me up in front of Princess Suzanna like that?'

'It's nothing to do with you fancying Her Royal Highness. It's your fear that's doing it.'

Percival stamps the ground, and shouts, 'Know-it-all! Are you saying the wasps fancy me?'

'No, of course not.'

'Thank Cosmo for small mercies. Well, hurry up then. Tell me what I should do.'

'Stand still as a statue. Close your eyes so you can't see the nasty pests. Keep your mouth closed. Take some deep breaths. Count four in. Hold for four. Count four out. Repeat the cycle for as long as it takes.'

The wasps start to leave him, one-by-one. 'Have they gone?' asks Percival, his eyes still shut.

'Yes, but you ought to stay as you are for a few minutes, in case you catch sight of them in the distance and get in a panic again.'

'If you say so.'

Noah leaves Percival and hurries over to talk to Goldie. For Darren's benefit, he bows to her. 'Good afternoon, Your Royal Highness. I trust the wasps haven't upset you.'

'Not at all, brave hero.' She winks at him and tips some champagne down the front of her dress—it seems, on purpose. 'Oh drat, how clumsy of me. Seveej, fetch me a cloth, would you?'

The butler rushes forward with the linen cloth he uses as part of his champagne-serving ritual.

Goldie waves him away. 'No, that will not do at all, Seveej. You cannot possibly use your serving cloth on royalty. I must have a brand-new towel that has never been used before.'

'What's going on over there?' calls out Percival, keeping his eyes closed. 'I do hope Noah isn't causing trouble, Princess.'

'No, of course not, he is a perfect little gentleman,' she replies. To Noah, she mutters, 'unlike a certain pretentious poodle, who hasn't the first idea how to address royalty—"Princess", I ask you, as if I am the plumber's girlfriend.'

'You're very good at acting the princess.'

She gives Noah a playful pinch. 'That is because I *am* a princess, you numbskull, but sometimes being in the public eye gets too stressful for me and my hair falls out. Have you never come across a bald princess before?'

'Not personally, but I'm sure they exist in one universe or another.'

'Can I open my eyes yet?' asks Percival. 'My sting is hurting. Is someone going to do something about it?'

'You need to keep your eyes shut for at least five minutes more,' says Noah, 'until we're sure all the wasps have gone home.'

'Shall I get some vinegar for the sting?' Darren asks, with a wink.

'What an excellent idea,' Noah replies, aware that sloshing vinegar on a sting after all this time will not work as the venom will have penetrated Percival's skin too far. The best remedy to cool off his pain is right next to him: ice cubes in a champagne bucket and a cloth to wrap them in.

Noah sits down next to Goldie. He gets straight to the point. 'How are you going to help me to get out of here with Bluebell?'

'By fussing around the poor patient prettily and letting him think it's the start of a wonderful romance.'

'Yuck.'

'Don't worry. I'll make my excuses before he's fully recovered from his wasp attack.'

182

'Apart from you, who else can I trust?'

'My old friend, General Reggie Basset. He's won many a battle in his time. Follow his orders, and all will be well.'

The poodle-man shouts at them, his eyes still squeezed shut. 'What are you two jabbering on about? The wasps must have gone by now. Where's the vinegar? Is your dress dry? What's happening?'

Goldie mutters to Noah. 'Return to Reggie. Leave the patient to me.'

Back on the terrace, the General passes Noah a fresh cup of tea and urges him to eat some more cakes to keep up his strength. This is the first Noah has heard about cakes having such a beneficial effect. He wolfs down five cupcakes and six marzipan fruits without complaint.

Goldie has guided Percival to sit on the bench next to her, where she administers first aid to him. This involves feeding him sips of champagne from his glass, while holding an icepack to his neck. By the glazed expression on his face, it seems the pain is worth the result.

<><><>

From the chestnut avenue comes the sound of R'n'B. The music reminds Noah of Phil Labrador's previous two street-dance demos on the night of their big escape from Roomdaorb and, later, in the Arbordral of Faces. Then Noah thinks of a conversation of a week ago, when Darren asked 'the gardener' how his routine was going, and it all falls into place.

Reggie Basset wears a serious expression on his face—his facial wrinkles, long rust-coloured ear leathers, and plush white dewlaps all weighted down by gravity— but he's busy tapping to the R'n'B rhythm under the

183

table with one of his paw-feet. 'Shall we wander over there?' he says, not waiting for a reply. With military precision, he positions his dome-shaped cap on his head and marches off at the speed of a military quickstep.

Noah rushes to keep up with him, noting how respectfully the other guests open a path to let them pass. They arrive in time to see Phil Labrador run towards a chestnut tree, walk several steps up its trunk, rotate his feet around ninety degrees, push himself off the trunk, and do an impressive spin in the air. When he lands on his feet, he does a back flip while running forward. From here, he does a Zyx version of drops, floor rocks, rollbacks, hand hops, backspins, elbow spins, and head spins.

His gear is something to behold. He wears a white bandana with green spots; a close-fitting sleeveless emerald-green vest with Percival Poodle's logo on it; emerald-green armbands; beat-up white jeans with holes in them, and emerald-green basketball shoes.

Everyone claps and cheers all his moves, apart from a group of middle-aged spaniel-women wearing big hats and floral dresses with plain linen tailored jackets. These particular females frown and purse their lips like cross teachers on duty at a school dance. They are an open invitation to anyone wanting to shock them, and this is just what Phil does next. The music ends, he lands on both paw-feet with his back to the spaniel-women, and fetches his tail out of his trousers to give it a good wag at them.

'Arrest him!' they shriek in unison.

The audience doubles up with laughter. Jimmy Whippet is in the middle of it all. 'It ain't illegal,' he yells, 'since the Boss don't mind it, and he *is* the law.'

Phil goes right up to one of the spaniel-women,

184

turns his back on her again, and tickles her nose with the end of his tail before returning it to his trousers. As she crumples to the ground in a faint, her companions cluck around her and berate the other guests for their lack of consideration.

'Stupid woman,' mutters the General.

'Do you know her?' Noah asks.

'Yes, that's Charity, the ex-wife of one of my former officers, Stark. He started out such a brilliant fellow, until taken in by that swooning ninny. Thence ruined and turned rogue, he has taken to wearing pink, beating out rhythms with a stick, and calling himself a Lieutenant.'

Phil glances down at Charity with a snigger. He dons some dark shades and a hooded sweatshirt. With a swaggering gait, he walks up to the General. 'Hi Reggie, old mate, how goes it?'

The General exchanges a high five with the street-kid, followed by a loud haw-haw of a laugh. 'Fascinatingly well, Philip, all things considered. And I don't need to introduce you two, do I?'

Phil high fives with Noah, too. 'Mate, your ability to survive this place is awesome. And your patience is about to be rewarded. When that psycho unwraps his prezzie, you'll be out of here, pronto.'

'Forget it. I'm going nowhere without Bluebell.'

'It's all in hand. Trust me.'

'Who's the present from?'

'Professor Watson, of course.'

'Well, *of course*, indeed. Who else, other than that hateful, double-crossing, lying witch?'

'Forget her, mate. In a little less than ten minutes, all hell will break loose.'

185

CHAPTER SIXTEEN

Special Delivery, Courtesy of Zyx's Parcel-Force

All the guests assemble on the lawn by the marquee. They chat amongst themselves until Monsieur Percival Poodle appears with Her Royal Highness Suzanna upon his arm. He and the princess sit down side-by-side upon high-backed chairs and an expectant hush falls over the crowd.

'We go through this ritual every year,' Jimmy whispers to Noah.

He hisses back at him. 'You'd know, considering you're in the Poodle's pocket. And what was that wristwatch stunt of yours about?'

'It's called playing the enemy for your friend's sake.'

'Taurus plop,' says Noah, a little too loudly. General Basset taps him on the shoulder and shushes him.

Several minutes pass by, the quiet so intense that an ant would have trouble crossing the lawn unheard. Just as Noah thinks the silence will never end, some bagpipes start up on the terrace, almost giving him a heart attack.

186

The General lets out a great sigh. 'In the name of Cosmo, the unconquerable, our host is such a hypocrite. All this pomp and circumstance, when he's so anti-establishment.'

Phil Labrador digs Noah in the ribs and gives him a wide grin. 'You ever heard of the expression "vanity before calamity"?'

'Pride before a fall, you mean?'

'Yeah, I guess.'

The piper blasts out some horrid tune resembling a national anthem. Noah pins back his ears against the noise, hoping to protect his eardrums from rupture. The assault ends on a deafening blast, heralding the arrival of the postal delivery dog-man.

Lord Hamish MacScottish Terrier, who's dressed in full postal worker uniform, pushes a trolley upon which stands a box secured by white ropes. The box is about a square metre in size and has a ventilation pipe emerging from its top. He brings the trolley to a halt in front of Percival and lifts his cap to salute him. 'Your package, Moss-your.'

The poodle-man scowls at him. 'Are you sure it's the right one?'

'Of course it is, Moss-your. This *is* Le Château Blanc et Somptueux, is it not?'

'You geriatric old fool, everyone from one end of the kingdom to another could answer that question.'

Her Royal Highness pats Percival's arm. 'Oh please, dearest, the suspense is killing us. Be a darling and open your parcel. We want to admire this year's addition to your esteemed collection.'

Percival replies in a whiny, petulant voice. 'But I was expecting something bigger, my sweetness. I cannot stomach disappointments. They are likely to bring on

187

one of my severe attacks of indigestion.'

A scrabbling and scratching noise starts up inside the box, which is accompanied by another sound that's familiar to Noah but produces a puzzled frown upon the poodle-man's face, as well as upon the faces of many of the guests.

'But it's not meant to do that,' says Percival.

The princess pats him again. 'How can you know the voice of a unique creature in advance?'

'My supplier sent me a video of it, and it certainly didn't yowl like that. More a barking and a huffing sort of animal it was.'

'Perhaps the video just had poor sound quality. Come on, dear Percival, everybody is waiting.'

'You there,' he calls out to the postal delivery dog-man, 'put that package onto the ground, untie those ropes, and wait whilst I check if the creature has arrived in one piece, so I can sign for it.'

Lord Hamish's eyes cross and his jaw visibly clenches. Doubtless, he's fighting a strong desire to savage Percival, but he does as commanded.

Percival walks up to the package and clicks his paw-fingers at Seveej. 'Hey, stuffed-shirt, you—scissors to the ready.'

Beneath the brown paper wrapping there's shiny emerald-green paper tied with white satin ribbon. This strikes Noah as strangely decorative considering the unpleasant yowling coming up through the ventilation pipe. Percival tears off the paper, leaving only the cardboard box to open. He takes the scissors from Seveej and, with his paw-hand shaking, cuts a jagged route through the parcel tape while holding the top of the box in place.

With the last snip, the General says, 'On your

188

mark, get set, go!'

◇◇◇

Something black and white bursts out of the box, with all four sets of claws not heading for the ground but straight for Percival's face.

He cries, 'That's no panda!' and tries to hide behind the princess.

Indeed it's not a panda but something far more extrovert that seems to strike fear into the hearts of all those present. As the guests break into a stampede, it dawns on Noah that this is the first time he's come across this species of creature since arriving in this dimension. How could he have overlooked the absence of something so common in his world? Then again, he has always much preferred dogs to cats, so why miss them when they're not there? For the first time in his life he's overjoyed at the sight of a domestic cat: better still, a large, ugly black and white tom in a temper.

'Go!' yells the General and Phil in unison.

Noah stays put, gripped by the sight of Seveej extracting the tom's claws from his master's face. The butler holds the wheeling creature out in front of him and tries to shove it back in its box. It wriggles free, hissing and spitting at him, and bites his paw-hand before making a dash for the marquee. Gauging by the loud cries of dismay coming from the catering staff in the marquee, it's clear the enraged tomcat is demolishing tables full of posh grub.

Jimmy Whippet flies past Noah, grabbing him by the arm as he goes, and shouting. 'You wanta end up pickled, or what?'

'Whippet … thief … stop,' calls out Percival. 'That's my property you're purloining.'

Phil Labrador sprints up behind Noah and snatches

189

at his other arm, propelling him along.

From behind, Percival lets out a shriek of fury. He follows this with words that slice into Noah, sharp as a hurled sabre. 'Chantelle's for the glass box.'

Noah battles to wrench himself free, but Phil and Jimmy have him locked in their tenacious grips. The three of them catch up with the stampede and they become part of one great surging entity. From round the corner of the château by the entrance to the cellars, Noah sees Hamish MacScottish Terrier charging along with his trolley (complete with cardboard box) and disappearing with it into the shrubbery.

They arrive at the main gates, only one of which is open. Everyone is trying to get through at once, which causes such a jam that nobody gets through at all. This gives two security guards the chance to frisk the guests in case they've pocketed any of their host's valuables.

Noah is glad of the jam. 'I'm going to rescue Bluebell.'

'Not while I'm in command, you won't,' says General Basset from behind him.

Noah stomps on Jimmy's paw-foot, elbows Phil in the stomach, and manages to break free. He sprints over to the front door of the château and stops dead, feeling a complete idiot for not having a plan in his head. This doesn't stop him attempting to get inside the building; he's both furious and desperate. When the door refuses to budge, he attacks a window with a chunk of cement broken off a drain's gulley surround.

After going at the window with all his might for a minute, he decides it has reinforced glass. This makes him in an even worse rage. He storms up and down the frontage, hot enough to spontaneously combust, and shrieks insults at Percival, demanding his immediate

190

arrest for illegal trade of alien species, false imprisonment, cruelty to animals, and murder.

In the midst of his tirade, an upstairs window opens and out pops Darren's head. 'Shut it, Noah, or I'll shoot you.'

Noah stops shouting and glares up at him. 'You wouldn't dare.'

'Don't put me to the test. Just leave, okay.'

This does Noah's head in. What is Percival's chief security guard doing ordering him to go, when he's duty-bound to recapture him? 'Stop confusing me. It's not okay. I'm not going anywhere without my dog.'

Darren waves his gun at Noah. 'You take me for a moron? Beat it now, before I'm forced to blow your brains out.'

'Blow them out then, and stuff me in a glass case for all I care. Name it *Alien Exhibit with a Hole in its Head*. Either you're deaf, or you haven't heard me. I am not leaving, unless it's with my dog, you hear me? Not … not … not lea—'

A bullet whistles past Noah's ear, grazing the tip of it. It stings worse than hell.

At the sound of the shot, the surging crowd at the gate panics. It overpowers the security guards there and squeezes itself through the exit as a singular entity until the drive is empty, apart from two beaten, trampled, and stunned security guards. Even General Basset, Phil Labrador, and Jimmy Whippet have vanished.

'Last chance!' hollers Darren.

With hot tears in his eyes and the bitter guilt of failure burning in his heart, Noah jogs past the dazed security guards at the gate and heads off down the hill away from Bluebell, condemning her to almost certain death.

<>< ><>

Rounding a bend in the road, Noah looks down the hillside and sees Lord Hamish MacScottish Terrier pushing his trolley at high speed towards Nod Nol City. At the same time, about thirty heavily armed dog-men, with snouted balaclavas covering their faces and dressed in black from head to foot, storm up the hillside towards the château. Guessing from their size and demeanour, they are out for blood.

It's too late to hide, so Noah stays standing there in the middle of the road with his eyes closed tight, expecting the worst. Their boots thunder on the tarmac; Noah's thumping heart races them. Everything vibrates, around him and inside of him. It's as if a monumental earthquake is about to take out the whole dimension. Terrifying as orcs, the armed dog-men chant in one united, aggressive voice and continue on their relentless advance closer, and closer, and closer, and...

They part ranks and pass him by, still chanting. Not one of them acknowledges his presence there. He opens his eyes and turns to watch their final ascent to the château. Darren and the General stand outside the gate in the road. The General exchanges a salute with the first of the armed dog-men to arrive, and the troop continues on inside.

Lord Hamish MacScottish Terrier and his trolley have disappeared out of view below. Gunfire sounds above. And Noah has no idea what to do next. Should he hang about to see what happens at the château and maybe find a way to liberate Bluebell?

Darren yells down the hillside at him, 'Head for the park!'

'What park?'

'The large green area, east of the city. You can't

miss it.'

'Grass? Trees? The real deal?'

'Just go. Now.'

'What about my dog?'

'The park, NOW!'

'But I look like a boy.'

'Just keep running.'

'What about my dog?'

Darren throws up his paw-hands in the air in despair. 'Go!'

Although Noah caught a glimpse of the park from up the top of the hill, now he has reached the bottom of the hill the park is no longer visible. He's lost: a stranger in a strange land who stands out from the natives like a sore thumb.

A group of pit-bull-youths hang out on a street corner, doubtless waiting to reclaim their night turf when the offices close. One of them shouts 'baldy' at Noah.

Noah keeps running.

A skinny and undernourished terrier-man, in a crumpled suit and loosened tie, stands in the doorway of an office, puffing on a roll-up that droops in the middle. He throws Noah a bored look amidst a cloud of smoke.

Noah keeps running.

A mongrel-street-cleaner sweeps the gutter. 'Ev'ning,' he says, without wasting extra effort in looking up from his work.

Noah keeps running.

A group of giggling dog-girls—Yorkshire terriers, Pekingese, and Afghan hounds dressed like secretaries— share gossip with each other while making eyes at the pit-bull-youths, who act all cool and ignore them.

Noah keeps running.

At the entrance to the subway stands a tall Saluki-girl, wearing hot pants, a sequin top, and stiletto heels. She smiles and waves at Noah. 'Howdy. Long time, no see.'

He skids to a halt and does a double take. 'You were in my stepmother's dressing room.' His accusation hangs there, with questions stacked up behind it.

Saluki-girl waggles her paw-finger at him. 'Oh, dear me, that naughty little four-leg of yours. Your stepmother must have been so, so, so, so cross.'

'What were you doing there?'

'Nicking things for my wardrobe.'

'Aren't there any decent clothes in your own dimension?'

'Where's the sport in that?'

'Is it your fault I ended up here?'

'Yes and no.'

'Thanks.'

'I have a good excuse,' she says, without apparent shame. 'That mouthy scallywag Jimmy Whippet told Percival Poodle that I'd jumped dimensions without any physical changes to my skin, fur, or eyes. He also threatened to snitch on me to my hubby, which would've meant the end to my clothes allowance.'

'What's this obsession with clothes? I don't get it.'

'Don't try. It's complex.'

'So why didn't Jimmy spill the beans to hubby?'

'He wouldn't have profited financially from it, plus he'd heard Professor Watson was ~~having difficulty~~ keeping up with Percival's demands for harder to obtain species of aliens.'

'Clothes. Money. Kidnap. Murder. How's your conscience?'

'I know it's wrong. Look, I'm really sorry. I didn't realise Percival killed the specimens when he got bored with them, nor did Phoebe. And she didn't intend for your four-leg to come with you.'

'You don't look very sorry. You'll have to do better than that.'

'The park ... you mustn't be late for your appointment.' Saluki-girl links arms with him. 'Come on. Trust me.'

'Why would I do that?'

'Because you're lost and you stand out like a sore paw-thumb. And because I'm under orders to get you to the park in one piece.'

<><><>

Now the workers have gone home, the clean white city becomes an underworld filled with dodgy characters.

Suki-Jane Saluki purchases a large bag of biscuits from a street seller near the subway, after which she points out to Noah some anorak-clad dog-people with mangy wolf faces lurking about in the shadows. 'If they approach you, offer them a biscuit, or they'll eat you.'

A merchant-dog attempts to interest the saluki-girl in selling Noah to him. 'How much do you want for him? I've a rich client. She suffers from asthma and needs a servant that doesn't shed hair.'

Suki-Jane looks interested for a moment, most likely thinking about all the clothes she could buy with the money, but she resists temptation. 'He does shed hairs—exceptionally long ones.'

The merchant retreats into the shadows, to be replaced immediately by a white-with-brown-spots dalmatian-man in a top hat, carrying a whip. 'Hey, gorgeous, I'll pay you good money for that oddity you're hanging out with. He'd be just the ticket for the freak

195

show in my travelling circus.'

'You want him to puke up all over your caravan? He suffers from travel sickness.'

Noah is both impressed and suspicious of Suki-Jane. She appears so calm and streetwise leading him through this underworld of dodgy characters, but he guesses this is why Reggie Basset has entrusted him into her care. 'How do you know the General?' he asks her.

'Through my partner, Jimmy Whippet.'

'I thought you were married?'

'St Cosmos, forbid! Not that sort of partner. We just work together.'

'Are you a thief?'

'More of a freelance spy who thieves when necessary.'

'Cool.'

They walk for an age not talking, apart from Noah occasionally inquiring how much longer it is to the park. Suki-Jane replies 'soon', or 'be patient', or 'stop asking' or 'I'll tell you when we're there', sounding more and more snappy each time. When he changes his line of questioning to 'are we lost?' followed by 'am I going to die?' she chucks a stick of gum into her mouth to chew on, and tells him, '*Sh*ub-up, *sh*upid boy.'

At twilight, they step from the suburbs (full of artificial greenery) into a narrow country lane with real trees and real grass verges. It smells so sweet after the sterility of the city. An owl cries somewhere off to their right. Noah looks in the direction of the sound as its silhouette sweeps across the face of the ascending moon just above the treetops.

Suki-Jane quickens her pace while Noah hobbles as best he can to keep up, his calf-muscles knotted and his feet blistered. Puffing like an old man, he asks, 'How can

196

you walk at such a speed on those towering, spiky heels?'

Without comment, she kicks off her shoes into a bush at the side of the lane and leaves them there. In her bare feet, she has shrunk at least ten centimetres. They carry on about another kilometre, their moon-silver path dappled with tree shadows, each step they take, removing them further from Bluebell. Noah's eyes start to fill with tears. She's most likely dead by now, he thinks, without him having had the chance to say goodbye to her properly.

Suki-Jane snatches hold of him, jolting him out of his morbid thoughts; she drags him to the side of the lane and across a dry ditch. They squat behind some bushes where it's too dark to see a thing. 'Shush,' she whispers in his ear. Her breath smells of peppermint.

From nearby, twigs snap. Someone lets out a sharp whistle. Another whistle comes from further off, followed by a short bark. Suki-Jane spits out her gum and whistles, too, three times in quick succession. More twigs snap, followed by the crunching sound of feet running at speed through the adjoining woodland.

'Follow me,' says Suki-Jane.

They leave the cover of the bushes and charge down a footpath, sending a family of rabbits dashing for the undergrowth. The footpath ends abruptly at a high wire fence, with dense ferns and felled trees beyond. It looks like the sort of place a murderer in a crime movie would dump a body.

Suki-Jane sits down on a big log. 'We have to wait here. … Not a peep from you, if you don't mind.'

He does mind, but thinks it futile to say so, considering he's doomed. Even the sight of an old badger coming out to forage a few metres away fails to

197

excite him. He watches the moon rise high in the sky, while his backside turns numb from staying still for so long. His throat, mouth, and lips are dry as old bones. He closes his eyes, exhausted.

Suki-Jane digs him in the ribs as he nods off. 'It's time. They're ready.'

'Who's ready?'

'Come. You'll see.' She takes him by the hand and leads him along by the fence, until they arrive at an iron gate loosely hooked together with an unfastened padlock. She opens the gate, pushing him through ahead of her. Once they're both inside, she puts the chain back and clicks the padlock shut.

'How are we going to get out again?' he asks.

'All you need to know is that we've arrived at the park and it's closed to the public until sunrise.'

— CHAPTER SEVENTEEN —

A Maze and a Conversation to Amaze

The park is a mix of neat lawns, rockeries, shrubberies, and walled gardens, interspersed with overgrown, wild areas. Ahead, Noah sees a tall stone tower with numerous windows, which appear lit up with electric light from rooms beyond, but close up it's just a folly consisting of a single wall with glassless window-slots through which the moon is shining.

Beyond the folly, he and Suki-Jane pass through a gap in a dense coniferous hedge clipped to perfection with box-like straight edges. Noah expects this to lead to another open area. Instead he finds himself walking along a grassy path with more of the same coniferous hedge on either side of it.

'Stay close,' says Suki-Jane, 'and don't utter a word. We're in a maze and I need to concentrate.'

They wander around for an age, the noise of Suki-Jane's gum-chewing slurps amplified by the intense quiet around them. After another complete circuit of the maze—or that's what it felt like—she starts muttering to herself. 'Bother, bother, bother, and bother. I'm late, I'm

199

late for a very important date.'

No time to say hello, thinks Noah.

'Goodbye I'm late, I'm late, I'm late,' sing-songs a familiar voice from the other side of the hedge. Not the voice of the harmless White Rabbit from *Alice in Wonderland*—how Noah wishes—but a witch posing as a scientist. 'Well, some go this way, some go that way,' she purrs from behind him now. 'But as for me, myself, personally—'

He spins around to find nobody there: not even the Cheshire Cat whose words the witch has stolen. His body sprouts goose bumps.

'I prefer the short-cut,' says the witch, from the direction Noah was facing in the first place.

He turns back slowly, expecting her to have disappeared again, but this time she is there.

At sight of Phoebe Watson in the flesh, he raises his hands in horror and lets out a loud shriek. She looks like the ghost of someone who got lost in the maze and died there. To add to this, Suki-Jane is nowhere to be seen, which means one of two things: either she has cleared off, her mission complete, or Phoebe has killed her and thrown her over the other side of the hedge.

Fear, exhaustion, and confusion bind Noah to the spot; disconnected thoughts drift through his mind like broken cobwebs. Phoebe stands watching him, biding her time. He recalls the various descriptions dog-people have applied to her, such as, 'the worst fly-by-night character you ever could meet', 'old crone', 'fierce as a bear', and 'devilish'. This is the woman who can control the cranky and unpredictable hammock apes at the click of her fingers.

The sudden noise of a cricket's chirruping breaks Phoebe's spell over him. He charges off down the grass path and turns sharp-left through the hedge onto a new path, a surge of anger overriding the pain of his blisters. Phoebe whizzes after him on bare feet, her movement as nimble and quick as a racing ferret. She attempts to grab him, but he sidesteps her and zigzags up the remainder of the path with her close at his heels. Her long shadow races ahead, eating up his shadow.

Another gap opens up in the hedge, this time to his right. Noah flings himself through it and lands on his hands, his chin missing the ground by a centimetre. He leaps to his feet and checks for damage, clenching and unclenching his fists and rotating his wrists. Nothing broken.

Taking off again, he glances back and collides with a hedge blocking his way. Dead-end. He spits out bits of bitter-tasting leaf and wood-grit from his mouth, aware of the last dregs of energy draining from him. His arms drop to his sides and he bends into a stitch, his heart jumping about in his chest so hard it makes him giddy.

Phoebe guards his only possible exit. She shuffles her feet and snatches a look at her wristwatch. Her fingers are restless. She's wearing her feather and bone necklace, which she keeps touching and stroking as if seeking reassurance from the individual trophies hung there.

'Well, go on then,' says Noah. 'If you're going to kill me, you'd better get it over with.'

She tilts her head to the left, her owlish face wrinkled in puzzlement. 'Why on earth would I want to kill you, Noah?'

'We're not "on earth". We're in Zyx.'

She parts her lips, showing the tips of her teeth in a smile of sorts. 'You've got to trust me, if you want to get out of this place alive.'

Noah considers yielding—her tone is gentle enough—but he spots something most disturbing about her jewellery. She's wearing a pink wooden high priest and warrior as earrings, and, amongst the trophies on her necklace are three purple wooden infantrymen. All five pieces are identical to the ones missing from Percival's Trap-set, and much too much of a coincidence.

Noah erupts in fury. He rips off her necklace, sending the pieces flying, and yanks one of her earrings from her ear, drawing blood. Her eyes water and she winces a little, but she doesn't make any move against him. He pummels her with his fists and shrieks at her. 'Your promises mean nothing! How dare you give my dog to Percival Poodle? Murderer. Evil scientist. I hate you, I hate you, I hate you. And all those other creatures, mutilated, stuffed. You knew they were for the knife, whatever Suki-Jane says. You should be in a glass case, not them.'

'I promise you, I'd no idea about Room 51 until Dorothy Dalmatian told me.' Her voice fades to a hush. She looks at the ground.

'But why do business with Percival at all?'

'He didn't give me much of a choice.'

'Why? How? Tell me.'

'Okay, but time's running out. We have to get going, now.'

'What's the hurry? Why are we in this maze?'

'You're young, nimble, and slippery. Cornering you in a maze seemed the best way to catch you.' She glances at her wristwatch again, and then looks up at the moon. 'We have one hour and eleven minutes to make it to the lake.'

'The lake? You can't get rid of me that easily. I'm

202

not going anywhere without Bluebell, even if she's in a glass case, and—'

'Just shut up until I tell you otherwise, please.'

'No.'

'Trust me.'

'Earn it then, by explaining yourself.'

They walk on a towpath alongside a moon-silvered stream, which Noah assumes leads to the lake, and Phoebe begins her story...

'When I was at university, my physics professor built a machine called "Time-worm", but decided it too risky to test. I got impatient with him, unable to see the harm in sending something small—a beetle—ten minutes into the future and back again. I broke into the lab and—'

'What's this got to do with Bluebell and me?'

'Just listen, would you? I typed in the correct co-ordinates on the computer but when I clicked SEND, freak lightning struck the university generators and transported me instead of the beetle. I landed up in another dimension, my journey unrelated to time-travel, and found myself in a containment cage inside Vermis Porta One. The controller of the space-lab, Dr Jason Cairn Terrier, was horrified when I appeared, and wanted rid of me before anyone saw me.'

'Why horrified? And what stopped him sending you back?'

'He'd been carrying out inter-dimensional jump trials himself—always to your city—but had rigged the results by failing to mention physical side-effects. The arrival of a human-turned-albino drove him into full-scale panic, especially as Zyx's Government hadn't licensed him to transport intelligent alien species. He

203

and his trial subjects had always crossed over during long electrical storms, giving them plenty of time to get there and back. But I'd arrived by a single bolt of lightning, so he was stuck with me, waiting on the British weather.'

'But I thought the Government here did whatever Percival Poodle told it.'

'Not then, it didn't.'

'He calls you his "old friend".'

'Friends with him? Never. When Borzoi dragged me off to Roomdaorb Hospital, Percival was serving a life-sentence for wiping the government computers with a virus, nicking all the back-ups, and shredding the paper records. Before his arrest, he chatted up the nanny who looked after the Prime Minister's pup-daughter and persuaded her to hide the computer back-ups inside the cot mattress. Later, she handed a letter to the Prime Minister, outlining Percival's demands.'

'But what did the Government do to upset him in the first place?'

'He was always picking fights with the other civil servants, so the Chancellor of the Exchequer sacked him from his job as a filing clerk.'

'But he told me he worked for the Stock Exchange.'

'That's the cover story he agreed with the Prime Minister, in return for her co-operation with him.'

Phoebe glances at her watch again, then up into the distance where a white bank of clouds, illuminated by the moon, has begun to build up in the dark-blue sky. She hunches her shoulders and quickens her pace. 'We need to hurry.'

Noah speeds up to keep pace with her. 'You were going to tell me about Percival's deal with the Prime Minister.'

'You have to understand he's a skilled manipulator. If he can't win through charming his way there, he'll stomp about like a cranky child until someone gives into his demands for a peaceful life.'

'Is that why you helped him steal my dog?'

'It's a bit more complicated than that. Percival selected fellow inmates who could prove useful to him on the outside. He promised to buy them their freedom, in return for their loyalty—patients such as the Lurchers, Tom, Mac, Stark, Salt, Watt, Dittle, and Pegleg, who were imprisoned for their part in a failed military coup.'

Noah's heart speeds up as he readies himself to ask his next question. 'Were Phil Labrador and Goldie Golden Retriever in-patients at the same time as Percival?'

'Yes, but only short-term.'

A cold shiver passes over him, stopping him in his tracks. 'So they've been working for Percival all along, whilst pretending to be my friends?'

'They *are* your friends. And Percival never guessed the bald patient in a fun fur—Goldie—was the beautiful Princess Suzanna suffering a nervous breakdown.'

Phoebe checks the time again. 'Thirty-five minutes, if we're lucky.' She links arms with Noah to speed him up.

'Thirty-five minutes to what? Why lucky?' He doesn't like the close feel of Phoebe. She's all bone, muscle, and no padding.

'Those clouds—they're bothering me.'

'They look okay to me. Not rainy or anything.'

They enter a forested area. Their path is in shadow, apart from the occasional pools of light making it to the ground through gaps between wide-trunked redwood trees and mature rhododendrons. The dense mat of fallen needles is springy beneath Noah's feet, and ferns grow in abundance to either side of him. They give off the rich smell of strawberries. He thinks to himself how easy it would be for Phoebe to bump him off and dispose of him here.

She takes up her story where she left off, her voice more sinister in the altered acoustics of the woodland. 'When Percival discovered an "alien" had been admitted to Roomdaorb, he went so manic he needed extra tranquillisers to stop him climbing the walls with excitement. After he'd calmed down, he told me he'd wangle my release from hospital, along with his, if I promised to supply him with aliens to collect.'

A shiver passes through Noah and his eyes prickle with sudden tears, as he recalls Bluebell's abduction in vivid detail. Phoebe's story sounds more and more like the sort of full confession a murderer makes before bumping off her listener. He banishes his tears, determined to stay sharp to her every move.

'At first I didn't take Percival's promise seriously,' she says. 'He kept boasting he'd soon be top of the kingdom's Rich List, which sounded quite insane, but I thought it safer to humour him. Then, to my amazement, the Prime Minister ordered Percival's release from hospital, to stop him sharing details of the Government's dodgy property deals with the newspapers. Shortly after this, rumours reached me that he'd taken over the portfolios and bank accounts related to these properties.'

Noah's mind is threatening to cave in under the weight of all Phoebe is telling him. He is aware of a big scream trapped inside him, keeping him going. If he were to let the scream out, he would deflate like a popped balloon, and lose all fight.

Phoebe carries on talking faster and faster, while jogging to keep up with her words. She's on a roll, confessing all. 'You see, Percival ended up owning every Government building in Nod Nol City. He took over the Law Courts, too, as the judges had been involved in the dodgy property deals, making it easy for him to secure mine and the Lurchers' release from Roomdaorb.'

The blood pounds through Noah's head. His throat is parched. He stops to lean into a stitch and grab a few deep breaths. Phoebe is too into her story to have noticed him falling behind. He considers for a moment running from her, but to where would he run? Anyway she's probably about to get to the important bit now, about Vermis-porta One. He hurries to catch up.

'Percival took over the Government-funded space-lab and put me in charge of it,' she says. 'He bestowed upon me the title of Professor, demoting Dr Jason Cairn to my assistant. Soon after, I procured his first specimens for him—a couple of corkscrew ducks. You might be interested to know, some alien seeds I removed from their feathers ended up as twelve-metre high trees in under a year.'

'And became the Arbordral of Faces, right?'

'Yes, correct. And at first Percival was thrilled with all the creatures I got for his collection. Then he got bored with them always being white, and told me he wanted creatures in interesting colours. Inspired by a list he'd stolen from Dr Cairn—a list of human children—he demanded I bring him such a specimen without rendering it albino.'

'But you didn't have to do what he said. He's just a stupid poodle who thinks he's master of the universe.'

'Yes, I did, or he would have had me locked up in Roomdaorb Hospital for the rest of my life.'

'A small sacrifice, considering what's happened to my dog.'

'Look, I'm truly sorry, but do you want the full story, or not?'

'I guess.'

'When you and Bluebell entered the dimension via Vermis Porta Two, I didn't tell Percival you'd arrived together. This gave Sergeant Salt the chance to earn the LIMS double commission for delivering two aliens as separate transactions. Salt intended to transport Bluebell to Percival first, and then collect you later from Roomdaorb Hospital. But when my informant Jimmy Whippet told me of your planned escape, I had my friend, Finn McDrool, bring you to me.'

'You lot remind me of the Mafia. Just one big happy family.' Noah hopes to *knife* her with his sarcasm.

'Look, once I got to know you and Bluebell, I did care about your fate, but I didn't know what to do to help you—not until Dorothy Dalmatian told me about the aliens in glass cases and I sent Percival a cat instead of a panda for his birthday. Can't say I envisaged the creature terrifying everyone half to death, though.'

'Yeah, random,' Noah says, more interested in his surroundings than hearing any more of Phoebe's silly ploys to win him over. They've just left the forested area and entered a large meadow, beyond which lies the lake. He shudders at the sight of the water stretched there before him. The chances of anyone saving him from drowning a second time are nil.

Phoebe continues to prattle on. She's telling him that, by now, Percival Poodle's château will have been raided by the SAS—the Special Alsatian Service—and his taxidermy specimens impounded as evidence of his illegal trading in alien species, and that they'll be coming for her, too, as a party to his crimes. But as far as Noah is concerned, Phoebe is speaking from a distant place. All he can focus upon is his impending death and the absence of Bluebell.

— CHAPTER EIGHTEEN —

Moon Jump

In the moonlight, the lake's wide expanse glistens with silver, except where overhanging weeping willows shroud the water in darkness. Further out, lily pads float above unfathomable depths where Noah is sure a watery grave awaits him. He shudders with foreboding. There's nothing here to reassure him of Phoebe's good intentions.

'Come on, don't just stand there,' she says, taking his arm.

He shrugs her off. 'What now, then, Professor who isn't a professor? You've just told me a grand story, and here we are by this vile lake beneath a vile pretend moon, with not a soul in sight and my puppy in a glass case in the possession of the SAS. Great! So how soon, exactly, will the High Court judges be sending you to a penal colony on the other side of the universe?'

'Okay, I hear you.' She looks down at her watch and then up at Vermis Porta One. 'We've got six minutes to make it to that hut on the other side of the lake, after which we've only four minutes to get you to the end of the jetty to make your jump, or you're stuck here for another year.'

He screws up his eyes and peers across the lake at the distant hut and jetty. 'I don't see a boat tied up there. How are we going to make the crossing in six minutes?'

'Five-and-a-half minutes now, to achieve it on foot.' Phoebe breaks into a trot, her hand clasping his wrist, urging him on. 'No boat. It would make waves and mess with Vermis Porta Two.'

'But it's just a reflection. How does it work?' he asks, his breath shortening and his chest clamping.

'By translocation.'

'In plain English, please?'

'Re-ordering of particles.'

'How?'

'Dr Cairn will send out a signal from Vermis Porta One that will be polarised by the water.'

'What does "polarised" mean?'

'I haven't time to give you a science lesson. Simply, it's related to light and limiting vibrations.'

'Well, whatever it is, that's me taken care of. But what about Bluebell?'

Phoebe jerks at his arm so hard that it almost pulls it out of its socket. 'No more questions. Just move it, or I'll drag you there kicking.

<><><>

They arrive at the hut. Noah's lungs, throat, stomach-muscles, calf-muscles are burning up; his whole body is on fire with running so fast under stress. He leans forward and presses his hands into his sides, then flops on the ground on his back, defeated, and stares up at the hard, white moon.

Without Bluebell, there's no point to anything: just

211

like when his mum died. *To have to go through all that grieving again.* Not that Bluebell was a replacement for her, but, in choosing to love a dog rather than another person, he'd managed to stay loyal to Mum's memory.

Phoebe is talking again, her voice coming from over by the shed.

Noah thinks to himself, when's that silly witch going to stop her pointless yakking? He can't even be bothered to sit up, let alone lift his head and check out what she's rabbiting on about: that is, until Fate flips a coin in his favour.

First he hears General Basset's voice and then an apparition blocks out the moon. This apparition has a pinkish-brown nose, a chocolate-coloured velvety face, and yellowish-green eyes. His very own Bluebell stands over him on all fours and starts to wash him back to life with her warm tongue, but Fate seems intent on flipping the coin back again.

The sound of gunfire reaches Noah's ears. He extracts himself from Bluebell and scrambles to his feet, almost choking with fear. Bluebell jumps around him in excitement. 'What now?' he shouts at Phoebe. 'Have they come for you?'

General Basset answers for her. 'If there's an exchange of fire, it's between the LIMS and the SAS. This means Percival Poodle has co-operated with the Alsatians during questioning and they know there are two specimens missing from the collection they've impounded.'

'Are you saying they're coming for me and Bluebell?'

Phoebe rushes up, grabs Noah by the hand, and pulls him towards the jetty. Bluebell gives chase, giving her warning bites, but Phoebe ignores her and pushes

212

Noah forward. 'Run for your life. When you get to the end, you must grab hold of Bluebell and jump into the moon's reflection.'

'What? Have you gone insane? I'll drown. I'm terrified of water.'

'Just do it. This time you *have* to trust me. No argument.'

With Bluebell at his heels, he thunders over the rickety planks. They creak and list beneath his feet.

'You've thirty seconds to go!' Phoebe calls out.

With only about one-and-a-half metres between Noah and the end of the jetty, war breaks out. Bullets whistle. Guns retort. Sergeant Salt hollers insults at the SAS. Phoebe screams something about a cloud. A bullet misses Noah by a millimetre and bounces off the end of the jetty. It skims across the water and cuts through the moon's reflection, setting it dancing. He freezes at the sight of the circle of light surrounded by cold darkness into which he and Bluebell must dive.

General Basset's voice booms out. 'In the name of Cosmo, jump, or you'll miss Dr Cairn's signal.'

Cloud-reflections pile into the lake. A sudden strong breeze picks up a sweaty strand of Noah's hair and wraps it about his face. Darkness creeps in, eating up the silvery light; clouds obscure half the moon.

Phoebe rushes up the jetty shrieking at the top of her voice. 'You're twenty seconds late already. If that moon disappears completely, you're—'

A bullet silences her, cutting her off in mid-sentence.

Noah grabs hold of Bluebell, and together they leap into the last quarter of the moon's reflection.

Down…

Down…

Down…

Down…

<><><>

Noah sinks into a dark enclosed space and collides with some kind of plastic float that he pushes away from him. Dazed and spluttering, he stands up in a solid plastic box full of water. It has a bottom, four sides reaching up level with his waist, and no top.

A sodden-coated Bluebell emerges from the water next to him. She climbs up on her hindquarters and rests her paws on the side of the plastic box.

Rubbing water out of his stinging eyes, Noah sees above him chinks of dim grey light poking through a solid expanse with cobwebs hanging from it. He wriggles his fingers about in his ears to clear them of water. Bluebell shakes her head.

Noah hears a sound. He knows Bluebell can hear it as well. She starts leaping about dementedly to escape the plastic box. *Co coooooo coo* goes the dove sitting above them, beyond the chinks of grey light. Noah peers into the gloom of his musty-smelling surroundings to get his bearings. The dust plays with his nostrils, trying to tease a sneezing fit out of him.

As his eyes adjust, dark sentinels transform into piled-up cardboard boxes. Along with these, there are stuffed-full black plastic bags, broken bits of furniture, discarded toys, a folded up silver Christmas tree, and suitcases. He blinks extra fast to make sure he isn't imagining things. But no, there it is, in all its glorious untidiness: the jumble of his attic back home. He guesses he and Bluebell have ended up in the water tank in the roof instead of his bedroom, having jumped into the moon late.

Bluebell wags her tail and laughs up at him, with an

214

excitable huffing-puffing-panting noise. Down on all fours now, she has a good shake out of her coat, at which point it dawns on Noah that he's standing in only a few centimetres of water, instead of the half-full tank of a minute ago. He holds Bluebell still, and smooths her down. 'Shush, a moment. Good girl. I need to think.'

When they first fell in the tank, the water level would have risen, possibly in enough quantity to make it spill out the top. As well as this, he mistook the ball cock for a float and bent it out of shape, adding to the chance of spillage. But now, even though water is still pouring in via the inflow pipe, the tank is almost empty, which means only one thing: it has a hole in it.

With this realisation, he vividly recalls his stepmother's temper: how small and ill it used to make him feel. She exists like dry rot in a corner of his brain. *Pull yourself together, Noah. You're bigger and braver, now. You've met far scarier characters than Kate is, and survived. You can reason your way out of this.* But how is he going to do so? His stepmother has absolutely zero imagination and no sense of humour. She's worse than Percival on that front. At least you could appeal to the poodle-man's vanity by telling him how brilliant he was.

Perhaps this is the way around Kate, too, but first he must explain what he's doing in the water tank in the attic with a full-grown Labrador retriever bearing only a passing resemblance to Bluebell the puppy. *Then again, what does he care, after all he's been through?*

The alarm clock goes off in his parents' bedroom. He hears someone going to the bathroom. It is Kate. She calls out something to Dad about the water level being low in the toilet and the taps not working. He tells her to stop moaning, go make some tea, and he will take a look at it when he has had a chance to wake up.

215

She opens the bedroom door and walks onto the landing. A drawn-out silence follows. She opens a second door. Noah braces himself for the banshee shriek, his heart speeding up a little, but not as much as it would have done in the past. The shriek rises up through the floorboards from the landing below him, trying to saw him in half without success. A string of expletives follow, on a par with one of Sergeant Salt's outbursts.

'Turn it down, girl,' Dad shouts at her. 'Give your old man a chance to wake up first.'

'No, I won't turn it down,' Kate shouts back at him. 'I told you *that* plumber was a cowboy when he didn't put a lid on the tank. And now it seems he didn't joint the pipes properly either.'

'What's the plumber got to do with my morning cuppa?'

'Forget tea, you moron. There's water pouring out of the roof hatch on the landing and the ceiling to my dressing room has just fallen in.' She lets out another scream—longer than the first—throws various objects around, and then states with surprising calm, 'My clothes are all ruined, and I want a divorce.'

Dad replies with equal calm. 'I'll take me torch and kill the stopcock, then.'

A minute or two later, the loft hatch opens. The ladder rattles and bangs into place, and Dad clatters up its rungs. His head and shoulders emerge through the hatch, followed by the rest of him. He shines his torch at the tank, jerks his arms, gasping, and almost topples back down the ladder. Bluebell, with her paws up on the side of the tank again, lets out a loud woof at him, either because she doesn't recognise him, or because she hasn't seen a man for ages. Dad climbs right up into the attic

216

and stands there speechless, with his mouth opening and closing but no words coming out.

Noah says the first thing that comes into his head. 'Sorry, Dad, I was abducted by aliens.'

Only Time Will Tell

Six months on, Noah hasn't become a celebrity, despite his insistence that aliens abducted him. It turns out that he and Bluebell spent the equivalent of a year in the Zyx-dimension, while only a few hours passed back home.

On the day he returned, Noah skipped school and Dad had time off work to buy him a larger school uniform, new shoes, and a replacement backpack. He also managed to persuade Noah to have a haircut, but only after an extended argument. Noah was rather fond of his shoulder-length hair.

Later, they took Bluebell for a walk in the recreation ground, where the other dog-owners gave them funny looks, although nobody went as far as asking Noah how he'd managed to grow from being a little squirt into a teenager overnight and why he'd replaced his puppy with an adult dog of the same name. Dad said they were probably being polite and British: either that or they feared for their sanity. But Bluebell's regular canine pals had none of the same problem recognising her.

At school, Noah got zero out of ten for a Spanish vocabulary test, having forgotten all the words he'd learned for homework a year ago.

Kate wanted to sell Noah's story to *News of the World* to help finance her new wardrobe of clothes and to become a media star, but Dad was dead-set against going public. He was afraid scientists would want to carry out horrid laboratory tests on Noah to check if aliens had genetically altered him. This made Kate all the more determined to turn their home into a media circus. In the end, Dad bought her silence by quadrupling her monthly clothes allowance and giving her all of the insurance payout related to the flood. After this, Kate stopped demanding a divorce.

These days, Noah writes out his homework by hand at home or uses the school computers in the library where it's too public for anyone to abduct him. Dad keeps asking if he would like a new laptop to replace the fried desktop one, but Noah always says 'no'; computers give him the jitters because they remind him of aliens.

Today, Dad has taken him to buy an electronic piano keyboard instead. This seems like a good enough idea, until Noah happens to look out of the showroom window and glimpses a woman crossing the street who looks alarmingly like Phoebe Watson dressed in white jeans and an emerald-green T-shirt.

Sarah Potter lives in Sussex by the sea with her husband, son, and chocolate Labrador. In the past, she worked in psychiatry. Nowadays, she writes quirky crossover novels and blogs about random things at http://sarahpotterwrites.com

A big thank you to my readers…

I really appreciate you taking time to read *Noah Padgett and the Dog-People*. If you enjoyed it, please could you (or whoever purchased my novel on your behalf) post a review on Amazon, book-related websites, and blogs, plus share about it on social media. Also, please recommend it to your friends, relatives, teachers, the school librarian, or anyone else you can think of—even the family dog! Once again, thank you.

This novel is enrolled in the Kindle MatchBook Scheme. It is also available as a free download on Kindle Unlimited or to borrow from the Kindle Lending Library.

Printed in Great Britain
by Amazon